I0571495

A Chain of Evidence

Carolyn Wells

A Chain of Evidence

Copyright © 2022 Bibliotech Press
All rights reserved

The present edition is a reproduction of previous publication of this classic work. Minor typographical errors may have been corrected without note; however, for an authentic reading experience the spelling, punctuation, and capitalization have been retained from the original text.

ISBN: 978-1-63637-834-3

CONTENTS

CONTENTS

I

THE GIRL ACROSS THE HALL

I do hate changes, but when my sister Laura, who keeps house for me, determined to move further uptown, I really had no choice in the matter but to acquiesce. I am a bachelor of long standing, and it's my opinion that the way to manage women is simply to humor their whims, and since Laura's husband died I've been rather more indulgent to her than before. Any way, the chief thing to have in one's household is peace, and I found I secured that easily enough by letting Laura do just as she liked; and as in return she kept my home comfortable and pleasant for me, I considered that honors were even. Therefore, when she decided we would move, I made no serious objection.

At least, not in advance. Had I known what apartment-hunting meant I should have refused to leave our Gramercy Park home.

But "Uptown" and "West Side" represented to Laura the Mecca of her desires, and I unsuspectingly agreed to her plans.

Then the campaign began.

Early every morning Laura scanned the papers for new advertisements. Later every morning she visited agents, and then spent the rest of the day inspecting apartments.

Then evenings were devoted to summing up the experiences of the day and preparing to start afresh on the morrow.

She was untiring in her efforts; always hopeful, and indeed positive that she would yet find the one apartment that combined all possible advantages and possessed no objectionable features.

At first I went with her on her expeditions, but I soon saw the futility of this, and, in a sudden access of independence, I declared I would have no more to do with the search. She might hunt as long as she chose; she might decide upon whatever home she chose; but it must be without my advice or assistance. I expressed myself as perfectly willing to live in the home she selected, but I refused to trail round in search of it.

Being convinced of my determination, my sister accepted the situation and continued the search by herself.

But evenings I was called upon as an advisory board, to hear the result of the day's work and to express an opinion. According to Laura it required a careful balancing of location and conveniences, of neighborhood and modern improvements before the momentous question should be decided.

1

Does an extra bathroom equal one block further west? Is an onyx-lined entrance greater than a buttoned hall-boy? Are palms in the hall worth more than a red velvet hand-rail with tassels?

These were the questions that racked her soul, and, sympathetically, mine.

Then the name. Laura declared that the name was perhaps the most important factor after all. A name that could stand alone at the top of one's letter paper, without the support of a street number, was indeed an achievement. But, strangely enough, such a name proved to be a very expensive proposition, and Laura put it aside with a resigned sigh.

Who does name the things, anyway? Not the man who invents the names of the Pullman cars, for they are of quite a different sort.

Well, it all made conversation, if nothing more.

"I wish you would express a preference, Otis," Laura would say, and then I would obligingly do so, being careful to prefer the one I knew was not her choice. I did this from the kindest of motives, in order to give the dear girl the opportunity which I knew she wanted, to argue against my selection, and in favor of her own.

Then I ended by being persuaded to her way of thinking, and that settled the matter for that time.

"Of course," she would say, "if you're never going to marry, but always live with me, you ought to have some say in the selection of our home."

"I don't expect to marry," I returned; "that is, I have no intention of such a thing at present. But you never can tell. The only reason I'm not married is because I've never seen the woman I wanted to make my wife. But I may yet do so. I rather fancy that if I ever fall in love, it will be at first sight, and very desperately. Then I shall marry, and hunt an apartment of my own."

"H'm," said my sister, "you seem to have a sublime assurance that the lady will accept you at first sight."

"If she doesn't, I have confidence in my powers of persuasion. But as I haven't seen her yet, you may as well go ahead with your plans for the continuation of the happy and comfortable home you make for me."

Whereupon she patted me on the shoulder, and remarked that I was a dear old goose, and that some young woman was missing the chance of her life in not acquiring me for a husband!

At last Laura decided, regarding our home, that location was the thing after all, and she gave up much in the way of red velvet and buttons, for the sake of living on one of the blocks sanctioned by those who know.

2

She decided on the Hammersleigh; in the early sixties, and not too far from the river.

Though not large, the Hammersleigh was one of the most attractive of the moderate-priced apartment houses in New York City. It had a dignified, almost an imposing entrance, and though the hall porter was elevator boy as well, the service was rarely complained of.

Of course dwellers in an apartment house are not supposed to know their fellow-tenants on the same floor, any more than occupants of a brown-stone front are supposed to be acquainted with their next-door neighbors. But even so, I couldn't help feeling an interest which almost amounted to curiosity concerning the young lady who lived in the apartment across the hall from our own in the Hammersleigh.

I had seen her only at a few chance meetings in the elevator or in the entrance hall, and in certain respects her demeanor was peculiar.

Of course I knew the young lady's name. She was Miss Janet Pembroke, and she lived with an old uncle whom I had never seen. Although we had been in the Hammersleigh but two weeks, Laura had learned a few facts concerning the old gentleman. It seems he was Miss Pembroke's great-uncle, and, although very wealthy, was of a miserly disposition and a fierce temper. He was an invalid of some sort, and never left the apartment; but it was said that his ugly disposition and tyrannical ways made his niece's life a burden to her. Indeed, I myself, as I passed their door, often heard the old ogre's voice raised in tones of vituperation and abuse; and my sister declared that she was not surprised that the previous tenants had vacated our apartment, for the old man's shrill voice sometimes even penetrated the thick walls. However, Laura, too, felt an interest in Miss Pembroke, and hoped that after a time she might make her acquaintance.

The girl was perhaps twenty-one or twenty-two, of a brunette type, and, though slender, was not at all fragile-looking. Her large, dark eyes had a pathetic expression, but except for this her appearance was haughty, proud, and exceedingly reserved. She had never so much as glanced at Mrs. Mulford or myself with the least hint of personal interest. To be sure, I had no reason to expect such a thing, but the truth is, I felt sorry for the girl, who must certainly lead a hard life with that dreadful old man.

Laura informed me that there was no one else in the Pembroke household except one servant, a young colored woman.

I had seen Miss Pembroke perhaps not more than a half-dozen times, and I had already observed this: if I chanced to see her as she

3

came out of her own door or descended in the elevator, she was apparently nervously excited. Her cheeks were flushed and her expression was one of utter exasperation, as if she had been tried almost beyond endurance. If, on the other hand, I saw her as she was returning from a walk or an errand, her face was calm and serene—not smiling, but with a patient, resigned look, as of one who had her emotions under control. At either time she was beautiful. Indeed, I scarcely know which aspect seemed to me more attractive: the quivering glow of righteous indignation or the brave calm of enforced cheerfulness.

Nor had I any right to consider her attractive in either case. It is not for a man to think too personally about a woman he has never met.

But I had never before seen a face that so plainly, yet so unconsciously, showed passing emotions, and it fascinated me.

Aside from Miss Pembroke's beauty, she must be, I decided, possessed of great strength of character and great depth of feeling.

But beyond all doubt the girl was not happy, and though this was not my affair, it vaguely troubled me.

I admitted to myself, I even admitted to Laura, that I felt compassion for this young woman who seemed to be so ill-treated; but my sister advised me not to waste my sympathy too easily, for it was her opinion that the young woman was quite capable of taking care of herself, and that in all probability she held her own against her poor old uncle.

"I don't see why you assume a poor old uncle," I said, "when you know how he berates her."

"Yes, but how do I know what she may do to deserve it? Those dark eyes show a smouldering fire that seems to me quite capable of breaking into flame. I rather fancy Miss Pembroke can hold her own against any verbal onslaught of her uncle."

"Then I'm glad she can," I declared; "as she has to stand such unjust tyranny, I hope she has sufficient self-assertion to resent it. I'd rather like to see that girl in a towering rage; she must look stunning!"

"Otis," said my sister, smiling, "you're becoming altogether too deeply interested in Miss Pembroke's appearance. She is a good-looking girl, but not at all the kind we want to know."

"And why not, pray?" I inquired, suddenly irritated at my sister's tone. "I think she is quite of our own class."

"Oh, gracious, yes! I didn't mean that. But she is so haughty and moody, and I'm sure she's of a most intractable disposition. Otis, that girl is deceitful, take my word for it. I've seen her oftener than you have, and I've heard her talk."

4

"You have! Where?"

"Oh, just a few words now and then—in the elevator perhaps; and one day she was talking to the agent who lives on the first floor of the apartment. Tumultuous is the only word to describe her."

"H'm; she must be of a tumultuous nature if she can't control it when talking to an elevator boy or a house agent."

"Oh, I don't mean she was then; but she gave me the impression of a desperate nature, held in check by a strong will."

"Sounds interesting," I said, smiling at my sister's vehemence.

"But that's just what I don't want!" declared Laura, emphatically. "You're not to get interested in that Pembroke girl; I won't have it! If you're going to fall in love at first sight, it must be with some one more gentle and more pleasing of demeanor than our mysterious neighbor."

"But you see, I've already had my first sight of Miss Pembroke, and so——" I looked at my sister, teasingly.

"And you've already fallen in love? Oh, don't tell me that!"

"Nonsense! Of course I haven't done anything of the sort! I've seen Miss Pembroke two or three times. I admire her beauty, and I can't help thinking that she is terribly treated by that cruel uncle. She may be a termagant herself—I've no means of knowing—but as a casual observer my sympathies are with her, and I can't help feeling hard toward the old man."

"You take a perfectly ridiculous attitude," Laura responded. "Like all men you are bewitched by a pair of big dark eyes and a pathetic mouth. I tell you, in all probability that poor old man is more entitled to sympathy than that melodramatic-looking girl!"

As I have said, I always humor Laura, even in her opinions; so I only responded: "Very likely you are right, my dear," and let the subject drop. I'm a lawyer, and I'm thirty-two years old, both of which conditions have led me to the conclusion that in dealing with women acquiescence in unimportant matters is always expedient.

But we were destined to become intimately acquainted with the Pembroke household, and to have opportunities to judge for ourselves whether Miss Janet deserved our sympathy or not.

The hall boy usually brought the first morning mail to our door at about eight o'clock, and when he rang the bell it was my habit to open the door and take the letters from him myself.

One morning I did this, as usual, and stood a moment looking carelessly over the letters before I closed the door. I may as well own up that I did this partly in the hope that Miss Pembroke would appear at the opposite door, where the boy was already ringing the bell. But my hope was unfulfilled, for, with a little click, the door

5

was pulled open, then suddenly stopped with a sharp snap by reason of a night-chain.

"Laws!" exclaimed what was unmistakably a negro girl's vice, "I nebber can 'member dat chain!"

The door was clicked shut again, and I could hear the chain slid back and released; then the door opened and the grinning face of the colored girl appeared, and the boy gave her the letters. As there was no further hope of catching a glimpse of Miss Pembroke, I went back to my breakfast.

II

THE TRAGEDY

It was perhaps half an hour later when I again opened my front door, to start for my downtown office. Laura accompanied me into the hall, as she often does and chattered a few parting inanities as we stood by the elevator. The car was rising, and as we are only on the third floor I had a half-formed intention of walking down the stairs, when the door of the other apartment flew open and Miss Pembroke ran out to meet the elevator. She was greatly excited, but not with anger, for her face was white and her eyes looked big and frightened.

Surely the word tumultuous applied to the girl now. But, it was plain to be seen that whatever caused her excitement it was something of importance. She had received a shock of some kind, and though she had herself well in hand, yet she was fairly trembling with almost uncontrollable emotion. She paid not the slightest attention to Laura or me, but clutched at the coat of an elderly gentleman who stepped out of the elevator.

"Oh, Doctor Masterson," she cried, "come in quickly, and see what is the matter with Uncle Robert! He looks so strange, and I'm afraid he's——"

She seemed suddenly to realize our presence, or perhaps she noticed the staring face of the elevator boy, for she left unfinished whatever she had been about to say, and, still clutching the doctor's coat, urged him toward her own door.

I did not presume to speak to Miss Pembroke, but I could not resist an impulse that made me say to the doctor: "If I can be of any assistance, pray call upon me."

There was no time for response—I was not even sure that the doctor heard me—but I turned back with Laura into our own apartment.

"Something has happened," I said to her, "and I think I'll wait a bit."

"Do," said my sister. "It may be that we can be of assistance to that poor girl; for if her uncle has a serious attack of any kind she will certainly want help."

I looked at Laura with admiring affection, for I saw at once that she had realized that Miss Pembroke was in serious trouble of some sort, and her true womanly heart went out to the girl, forgetting entirely her previous dislike and suspicion.

7

Almost immediately our door-bell rang, and, feeling sure that it was a summons in response to my offer, I opened the door myself.

Sure enough, there stood the elderly doctor, looking very much perturbed.

"You kindly offered your assistance, sir," he said, "or I should not intrude. I want immediate help. Mr. Pembroke is dead, Miss Pembroke has fainted, and their servant is so nearly in hysterics that she is of no use whatever."

Laura is always splendid in an emergency, so of course she rose to the occasion at once.

"Let me go to Miss Pembroke," she said, in her quiet, capable way. "I'm Mrs. Mulford, and this is my brother, Otis Landon. We are new-comers here, and do not know Miss Pembroke personally, but we are only too glad to do anything we can for her."

"Thank you," said the old gentleman, looking at Laura with an air of approval. "I'm Doctor Masterson, the Pembroke's family physician. I'm greatly surprised at this sudden death. I'm surprised, too, that Janet should faint away, for I have never known her to do such a thing before."

By this time we had all three crossed the hall, and were inside the Pembrokes' door, which opened into a short cross hall. On the right was the drawing-room, and here we found Miss Pembroke, who had not yet regained consciousness. She lay on a couch, and as the doctor bent over her she gave a convulsive shudder, but did not open her eyes.

"She'll be all right in a moment," said Doctor Masterson. "Janet is a plucky girl, and sound as a nut. I'll leave her in your care, Mrs. Mulford."

Laura was already hovering over the girl, and, with her intuitive womanliness, was doing exactly the right things.

The colored woman was crouched in a heap on the floor, and was rocking herself back and forth, with occasional wails.

"Stop that noise, Charlotte," commanded the doctor. "Don't make us any more trouble than we already have."

The command was not heeded, but without further comment he turned away from her, and as he beckoned to me I followed him from the room.

"I was at my wits' end," he exclaimed, "with those two women on my hands, and this dead man to look after!" As he spoke, we crossed the short hall and entered what was apparently the old gentleman's bedroom. I gazed with interest at the face of Robert Pembroke, and, save for what Doctor Masterson had told me, I should have thought I was looking at the face of a sleeping man. My first feeling was one of admiration, for the features were of classic mould, and the white hair, thick and rather long, waved back from a noble brow.

"What a handsome man!" I exclaimed involuntarily.

"Did you know him?" asked Doctor Masterson, looking at me keenly.

"No," I replied; "I've never seen him before. I've lived in this house but two weeks."

"Robert Pembroke was a handsome man," agreed the doctor, "but, with the best intentions, and with all the respect due the dead, there is little else good to be said of him. But his sudden death puzzles me greatly. I have been his physician for many years, and I should have said that he had not the least apoplectic tendency. Yet apoplexy must have caused his death—at least, so far as I can judge without a more thorough examination."

As he spoke Doctor Masterson was examining the body, and his look of bewilderment increased.

"He looks as if he were asleep," I said.

"That's just it," said the doctor. "There is no indication of a convulsive struggle or a spasm of any kind. His limbs are quietly composed, even relaxed, as if he had died in his sleep; which is not quite indicative of a stroke of apoplexy."

"Heart disease?" I suggested.

"He had no valvular trouble of the heart," said the doctor, who was continuing his examination. "He had gout, indigestion, rheumatism, and many ailments incidental to old age, but nothing organic, and I had supposed he would live many years longer to torment that poor girl in there."

"He was irascible, I know," I responded, feeling that I ought to say something.

"Irascible faintly expresses it," declared the Doctor, in a low voice; "he was cruel, domineering, tyrannical and of a brutal temper."

"And he vented it on innocent Miss Pembroke?"

"Yes; he did, though Janet is no patient Griselda. She can hold her own! I've known her to——"

Doctor Masterson ceased talking as he went on with his investigation.

A dozen questions rose to my lips, but I refrained from uttering them. Miss Pembroke's affairs were none of my business; and, too, the doctor was not definitely addressing me, but seemed rather to be talking to himself.

"Here's a key," he said, holding toward me a small bright key; "just take it for the moment, Mr. Landon, as it is doubtless an important one."

9

"Where was it?" I asked.

"On the bed, by Mr. Pembroke's side. It had probably been under his pillow. It looks like the key of a safety box of some sort."

I put the key in my pocket, with a pleased thought that it would give me an opportunity to speak with Miss Pembroke. Meantime I noticed that Doctor Masterson's attitude was becoming more and more that of a greatly perplexed man.

"I don't understand it," he muttered. "A man can't die without a cause. And every known cause shows its own symptom. But I find no symptoms. What can this man have died of?"

"No foul play, I hope," I observed.

"No, no; nothing of that sort! Mr. Pembroke died peacefully in his sleep. But how?"

Suddenly he straightened himself up with an air of resolve.

"Is there a doctor living in this house?" he asked.

"Yes," I answered; "there is one on the first floor. Shall I fetch him?"

"Do," said the old man. "Tell him that Doctor Masterson wishes to call him in consultation on a serious matter." I hastened on my errand, though not so rapidly as not to pause a moment to glance in at Miss Pembroke, who had recovered consciousness, and was lying quietly back on the sofa pillows, while Laura bathed her forehead with cologne. I well knew the soothing capabilities of Laura's finger-tips; and I also was not surprised to notice that the black girl had ceased her convulsive shuddering, and, though still sitting on the floor, was gazing at Laura as if fascinated.

All this I took in in a brief glance, and then ran hurriedly down the stairs in search of Doctor Post.

"Is this Doctor Post?" I asked as I entered his office.

"Yes," he replied, laying down the gloves and hat he held. Apparently, he was just about to go out, and I had fortunately arrived in time.

"Will you go up-stairs with me?" I went on. "Mr. Pembroke, on the third floor, is dead; and his physician, Doctor Masterson, is at a loss to discover the cause of his death. He sent me to ask you to join him in consultation."

"Doctor Masterson!" exclaimed Doctor Post, and I saw at once that the younger man was flattered at being called in consultation by the older and celebrated practitioner. "He wants me?" he asked, as if scarcely able to believe it.

"Yes; it is a peculiar case, and he asks your help. Will you go with me at once?"

"Certainly," and in another moment Doctor Post and I were in the elevator.

"Old Mr. Pembroke dead?" asked the boy as we entered.

"Yes," I answered briefly.

"Gee, is he? Well, I can't give him any weeps! He was sumpin fierce! He just put it all over that young loidy. Sometimes she'd come down in this elevator all to the teary, so's I 'most hadta order a consignment of weep-catchers for myself. She's a looker all right, and she sets off the house great, but she leads the dismal swamp life, an' that's right!"

I had neither time nor inclination then to reprove the boy for thus crudely expressing his opinion, for we had reached the third floor, and Doctor Post and I went at once to Robert Pembroke's bedroom.

I introduced the new-comer to his older colleague, and then turned aside while they consulted on the problem that faced them.

I was surprised that a physician of Doctor Masterson's age and experience should find it necessary to call the younger man to his aid, but as I knew little of medical men and their ways, I had no definite opinion on the subject. I felt a slight embarrassment as to my own presence in the room, but I also felt a hesitancy about returning to the drawing-room until the doctors should have reached a decision. I endeavored not to hear the low words they were speaking, but I couldn't help gathering that there was an element of mystery in Robert Pembroke's death. In order not to appear curious, I walked about the room, and idly noted its furnishings. Though not over-ornate, the appointments were comfortable and even luxurious. A great casy-chair stood by the window, which opened on an inner court, and which was in fact directly opposite the window of my own bedroom in our duplicate apartment. Near by stood a desk, open, and with its contents tidily arranged. The position of ink-stand, pen-racks and stationery proved the old gentleman to have been of methodical habits and orderly tastes. My lawyer's brain immediately darted to the conclusion that Robert Pembroke's sudden death had found him with his affairs all in order, and that his heirs, whoever they might be, would doubtless have no trouble in adjusting his estate. The dressing bureau and chiffonier presented just such an appearance as one would expect to see in the room of an elderly gentleman. While there were no fancy knick-knacks, there was a multitude of ebony-backed brushes and other toilet appurtenances. Moreover there were several bits of really good bric-a-brac, two or three bronzes, a carved silver box and some antique curios, that were evidently valuable.

Mr. Pembroke may have been quick-tempered and cruel-

11

natured, but he rose in my opinion as I noticed the good taste displayed in the furnishing of the room. However, this might be due to Miss Pembroke's housekeeping, and it somehow pleased me to fancy that it was.

Two scraps of paper or cardboard lay on the floor near the foot of the bed. Obeying my instinct for tidiness, and really without thinking of what I was doing, I picked them up and threw them into the waste basket. As I did so, I noticed they were stubs of theater tickets. I felt a momentary surprise at this, for I had been told that Mr. Pembroke never went out of the house. However, it was quite within the possibilities that the stubs represented Miss Pembroke's attendance at the theatre, or might even have been dropped there by some caller. These matters took no definite shape in my mind, but were mere drifting thoughts, when I heard Doctor Masterson say:

"Excuse me, Mr. Landon, but may I ask you to leave Doctor Post and me by ourselves for a few moments? This affair is assuming a very serious side, and it is necessary that a professional secrecy be observed, at least for the moment."

"Certainly," I replied, greatly awed by the apprehension clearly evident on the Doctor's kindly old face. "I have no wish but to be of service in any way I may, and I'm completely at your orders."

"Thank you, Mr. Landon," returned Doctor Masterson, courteously, "I will tell you that we have to deal with a very grave situation, but I will ask you to say nothing to the people in the other room concerning it."

12

III

JANET PEMBROKE

Leaving the two doctors to their consultation I went back into the drawing-room.

Although this room was the duplicate of our own living-room in the apartment across the hall, it presented quite a different appearance because of its richer furnishings. The simple tastes of my sister and myself did not incline us to velvet hangings and heavily upholstered furniture. Our whole room was lighter in effect, but the Pembroke drawing-room, while harmonious in coloring and design, was almost oppressive in its multitude of appointments. Tall pedestals supported large pieces of Chinese bronze. Embroidered screens made a background for high, carved chairs and inlaid tabourets. The rugs were antique and thick, the curtains conventionally draped and the pictures on the walls were paintings of value.

I instinctively felt that all of this reflected the old uncle's taste, rather than that of Miss Pembroke, for, though I had not seen her often, her general appearance had a note of modernity quite different from the atmosphere of her home.

I glanced at the girl as she sat beside Laura on the sofa. Though not a connoisseur in women's clothes, I am yet not so absurdly ignorant as many men are. Miss Pembroke wore a simple house dress of soft material and of an old rose color. There was a big black satin bow effectively attached somewhere—I can't describe its location, but it had broad streamers that fell gracefully to the floor. The simply cut garment and the soft dull color suited the girl's pale white complexion and dark hair. She was doubtless of an unusual pallor that morning, which made the thick curls clustering round her brow, and the big brown eyes seem even darker than usual.

It was late in October and a lighted gas log gave a comfortable warmth to the room.

Miss Pembroke seemed to be quite herself again, though still somewhat dazed, apparently, by what had happened. She showed no inclination to talk, but her manner was quiet and composed as she asked me to be seated. I had no wish to intrude, but I thought there might be other ways in which I could serve her, so I sat down and waited. There was an indescribable something in her manner, or rather in her appearance, that puzzled me.

I had thought her beautiful before, but in this time of sorrowful

13

emergency there was a mysterious expression on her face that gave her an added charm. She was not pathetic or appealing in effect, but seemed to be possessed of an energy and excitement which she determinedly suppressed. She showed no sign of grief at her uncle's death, but her calmness and self-control were unmistakably the result of a strong will power. Had she been broken-hearted, but for some reason determined that no one should know it, she would have acted this same way; but it also seemed to me that had she felt a secret sense of relief, even almost of gladness, at being released from the old man's tyranny, she must have acted much the same.

Occasionally her composure was broken by a sudden, quick gesture or an abrupt, impulsive remark.

"Charlotte," she said suddenly, "why do you stay here? You may as well go to the kitchen and go on with your work."

The black girl rolled her eyes apprehensively toward Mr. Pembroke's room, as if a superstitious dread made her hesitate.

"I don't like to go off my myse'f alone, Miss Janet," she said.

"But you must, Charlotte," said Miss Pembroke nervously, but not unkindly; "you must go and clear away the breakfast things."

"But yo' haven't had yo' breakfast, Miss Janet, honey."

"Never mind, Charlotte; I can't eat any breakfast. Clear it all away. I don't want anything."

I was much impressed with the tense, drawn expression of the speaker's face, and the quick, sharp accents of her voice, as if she had almost reached the limit of her self-control.

Here Laura interposed: "I'm sure, Miss Pembroke, you would feel better able to meet the day if you would eat something. Charlotte, if you will bring just a cup of coffee and a roll on a tray, I think Miss Pembroke will take some of it."

"Yas'm," said Charlotte, and, falling, as nearly every one did, into the way of obeying Laura's suggestions, she went away.

I endeavored to keep up the conversation by casual and unimportant remarks, and Laura ably assisted me, by responding to my observations. But though Miss Pembroke tried to join the conversation, it was impossible for her, and, as I had feared, her tense self-control gave way and she suddenly broke down in a fit of hysterical sobbing.

Laura tried to soothe her, but had sense enough not to try to stop her crying. She let the nervous and overwrought girl give way to her tears which of themselves brought relief.

"I didn't love him!" she exclaimed, her voice broken by sobs, "and that's why I feel so bad. I tried to love him, but he wouldn't let me. I honestly tried—don't you believe I did?"

14

She grasped Laura's hands as she spoke, and looked into her eyes.

"Of course I believe it," replied Laura, heartily; "don't think about that now, Miss Pembroke. I'm sure you have nothing to reproach yourself for."

"Oh, yes, I have. I'm a wicked girl! I ought to have been more patient with Uncle Robert. But he was so old and so cruel. He was my mother's uncle, you know, and he took me on sufferance—because he couldn't help himself—and he never let me forget it. He told me a dozen times a day that I was dependent on him for the bread I ate. And last evening we had a most awful quarrel! One of our very worst. Oh, I can't bear to remember it!"

"Don't remember it, dear," said Laura, with her arm still around the quivering body of the girl; "don't think of it."

"Think of it! I can never forget it. You see, he was determined that I should——"

Apparently Miss Pembroke had been about to make a confidant of Laura, when she suddenly remembered my presence. She straightened up with a start, and seemed to recover not only her poise, but the hauteur which I had so often observed in her demeanor.

It was a relief to the situation when at that moment Charlotte, the maid, returned with a daintily-appointed breakfast tray.

It was quite evident that the colored girl adored her young mistress. She hovered about her, arranging the tray on a small table at her side and looked at Miss Pembroke with an air of loving concern.

"Do try and eat sumpin, Miss Janet, honey; do, now."

"Thank you, Charlotte," and Miss Pembroke looked kindly at the girl; "I will try."

With a little nod, she tacitly dismissed the maid, but Charlotte lingered. After a moment of hesitation, she volunteered a suggestion, which was evidently weighing on her mind.

"Miss Janet, honey," she said, slowly, "ain' yo' gwine send fo' Master George?"

"George!" exclaimed Janet Pembroke. "Why, how strange I hadn't thought of it! Of course we must send for George. I'll telephone at once. You may go, Charlotte."

Again Charlotte left the room, and Miss Pembroke turned to Laura to explain.

"George," she said, "is George Lawrence, my cousin. He is my only relative except—Uncle Robert. He used to live with us, but a few months ago he moved to bachelor apartments farther downtown. If you will excuse me, I will telephone for him."

15

The telephone was in a small adjoining room, which was really rather a large alcove off the drawing-room. This was apparently a sort of music-room here, while my corresponding alcove—for the apartment was, of course, a duplicate of our own—I used as my smoking-room.

I heard Miss Pembroke, in a calm, clear voice, call up her cousin and ask him to come at once. She did not tell him what had happened. Then she hung up the receiver and returned to where we sat.

"I don't see why I didn't think of George sooner," she said. "I ought to have sent for him the very first thing."

"You were so dazed," I suggested, "that what would ordinarily be the most natural thing to do did not occur to you."

"Yes," she said, catching at my suggestion almost eagerly—"yes, that must have been it. I was dazed, wasn't I?"

"Indeed you were," said Laura soothingly. "You fainted quite away."

"Oh, yes," returned the girl; "that was when Doctor Masterson told me that Uncle Robert was dead. It was such a shock. I couldn't believe it, you know. Why, I never faint! I'm not that sort."

"Even so," said Laura, "the sudden shock was quite enough to cause you to faint."

The girl looked at her almost wistfully. "Yes, it was enough, wasn't it?" she said; "a shock like that would make anybody faint, wouldn't it? I just couldn't believe it. We—we never dreamed he would die suddenly. I wonder what George will say?"

"Is there any one else that you would like to have notified?" I asked.

"No," she said. "I have no other relatives at all. Of course we must tell Milly Waring, but I'll wait until after I see George."

"But aside from relatives, Miss Pembroke," I said, "is there no one else who ought to be notified? Ought you not to advise your uncle's lawyer?"

I was all unprepared for the effect this casual suggestion had upon the girl. Although she had recovered her composure almost entirely, it now seemed to desert her again. But instead of weeping her emotion was of a different nature; she seemed intensely angry. A red spot appeared in either pale cheek, and her dark eyes flashed fire. Her voice quivered when she spoke, but it sounded like the accents of suppressed rage.

"Uncle Robert's lawyer!" she exclaimed, in a tone of scorn; "he's the last person I want to send for!"

The words of themselves were astonishing, but not nearly so much so as the scathing inflection with which they were uttered.

16

"Then we won't send for him," said Laura, in her soothing way. "You shan't be troubled just now."

Laura looked at me with a glance of deep reproach, which was, to say the least, unjust; for, as a lawyer, it seemed to me I had made a most rational suggestion. Moreover, my sister's change of base somewhat surprised me. She it had been who denounced Miss Pembroke as being deceitful, melodramatic and untrustworthy! Now, she was not only befriending the girl as only one woman can befriend another, but she was resenting a most common-sense suggestion on my part.

But I was destined to learn that Janet Pembroke always did the unexpected.

As suddenly as it had come, her flash of anger left her, and with a quiet, almost expressionless face, she turned to me, and said: "You are quite right, Mr. Landon. I am sure it is a case where my uncle's lawyer should be called in. He is Mr. Leroy—Graham Leroy—and I suppose I ought to tell him at once about my uncle."

"You don't like Mr. Leroy?" I said, impulsively. Had I paused to think, I should not have spoken thus personally. But Miss Pembroke answered simply:

"No, I do not like Mr. Graham Leroy. But that does not make any difference. He has full charge of my uncle's financial affairs; and, too, he has long been his personal friend and adviser. So, I know it is right to send for him."

She sighed, as if her decision were entirely because of what she considered her duty.

It was absurd of me, to be sure, but I am always given to jumping at conclusions, and it flashed across me that Graham Leroy's interest in the Pembroke family extended farther than his professional relations with the old gentleman. I know him slightly, as a brother lawyer, and I knew that from a feminine point of view he was a most fascinating man. He was a bachelor, and though not young, was handsome, brilliant and exceedingly distinguished in effect. Moreover, flattering myself that I understood the contrariness of a woman's assertions in such matters, my mind leaped to the conviction that because Miss Pembroke had denounced him, she was in all probability in love with him.

And then I sternly inquired of myself how it could possibly matter to me if she were.

But this stern and questioning attitude of myself to myself did not deceive me in the least. I knew perfectly well that I was already sufficiently interested in Janet Pembroke to resent the introduction of such a dangerous factor as Graham Leroy into the case. Being a lawyer, the absurdity of my own mental attitude was perfectly clear to me, but being a man, I didn't care if it was. Of course, my sentiments toward her were nothing more than admiration for her beauty and sympathy for her sorrow. If these were augmented by the elusive mystery that seemed to enwrap her, that was an argument in justification of my sudden interest in a comparative stranger.

"Will you, Otis?" Laura was saying, and I collected my scattered wits with a start, as I said, "will I what?"

"Will you telephone to Mr. Leroy?" she said, a little impatiently, and I knew she was repeating her question.

"Of course," I said, jumping up and looking for the telephone book.

"His number is on the card by the telephone," said Miss Pembroke, and in a few moments I had Leroy's call. But he was not in his office, so leaving word for him to come as soon as possible, I hung up the receiver.

18

IV

DOCTOR POST'S DISCOVERY

A few moments after this, Mr. George Lawrence arrived. He let himself in at the front door with a latch-key, and walked into the room with the air of one familiar with the place.

"Well, Janet, what's up?" he began, and then, seeing strangers, paused expectantly.

"Mrs. Mulford," said Janet, "this is my cousin, Mr. Lawrence. Mr. Landon, Mr. Lawrence."

The new-comer bowed politely and with the graceful courtesy of a well-bred city man, then turned again to his cousin.

"I sent for you, George," began Janet, "because—because——"

But here her self-possession failed her, and she could go no further. She cast an appealing glance at me, as if to ask me to speak for her, then threw herself on the couch in an uncontrollable fit of weeping.

Laura sat beside the sobbing girl, while Mr. Lawrence turned to me for an explanation.

Judging at first sight that with a man of his type a straightforward statement would be the best, I told him in as few words as possible what had happened.

"Uncle Robert dead!" he exclaimed. "Why, what does it mean? He had no heart trouble that we knew of. Was it apoplexy?"

"I think so," I replied. "Two doctors are in there now, holding a consultation."

"Two doctors?" exclaimed Mr. Lawrence. "Who are they?"

"Doctor Masterson, who was, I believe, your late uncle's physician, and Doctor Post, who lives in this house."

"Which came first?" asked Mr. Lawrence.

By this time Miss Pembroke, who seemed to be subject to sudden changes of demeanor, took it upon herself to answer his question. She had stopped crying, and again showed that icy calmness which I could not yet understand.

"I sent for Doctor Masterson," she said. "I thought uncle was only ill, but when the doctor came he said he was dead; and then he wanted another doctor, so Mr. Landon very kindly went for Doctor Post."

"Why did he want Doctor Post, if Uncle Robert was already dead?" demanded Lawrence.

"To help him to discover what caused uncle's death."

19

"Then we must await the result of their consultation," he replied. He seemed about to say something else, but checked himself. I could readily understand why he should hesitate to say in the presence of strangers many things that he might have said to his cousin had they been alone.

I felt attracted to this young man. Although he had a careless, good-natured air, there seemed to be an underlying vein of kindly feeling and courteous solicitude. Like Miss Pembroke, he seemed to be controlling his emotion and forcing himself to meet the situation calmly.

George Lawrence was large-framed and heavily-built, while Janet Pembroke was a lithe and willowy slip of a girl; but their features showed a degree of family likeness, and the dark eyes and dark, curling hair were decidedly similar. They seemed congenial, and thoroughly good comrades. Miss Pembroke appeared glad that her cousin had arrived, and he seemed desirous of doing whatever he could to help her. I was struck by the utter absence of any expressions of grief on the part of either, and then I remembered what I had heard about the cruel temper of their uncle. Could it be possible, I thought, that these two were really glad rather than otherwise? Then I remembered Miss Pembroke's piteous weeping, and as I looked at Mr. Lawrence and noted his white face and clenched hands I concluded that they were both controlling their real feelings, and exhibiting only what they considered a proper attitude before strangers.

Then I began to think that since Miss Pembroke's cousin was with her, perhaps Laura and I ought to go away and leave them to themselves. I made a remark to this effect, but, to my surprise, both Miss Pembroke and her cousin insisted that we should stay, at least until the doctors had finished their consultation.

So we stayed, and Laura, with her usual tact, managed to keep up a desultory conversation on various unimportant subjects.

Occasionally the talk became more or less personal, and I learned that George Lawrence had previously lived with his uncle and cousin in this same apartment. It also transpired—though this, I think, was told unintentionally—that the reason why he went away to live by himself was because he could no longer stand the unpleasantness caused by the fierce fits of anger into which old Mr. Pembroke would fly upon the slightest provocation.

"It does seem a pity," he said, "that such a really fine man should be so utterly unable to control his temper. I could stand an ordinary amount of grumbling and fault-finding, but Uncle Robert in his rages was almost insane. He grew worse as he grew older. Janet and I lived with him for many years, and each year he grew

20

more unbearable. I suppose, poor old chap, it was his gout that made him so crusty and cross, but it kept me in hot water so much of the time that I couldn't stand it. Janet stood it better than I did, but she's a born angel anyhow."

Mr. Lawrence looked admiringly at his cousin, who acknowledged his compliment with a faint smile.

"I didn't stand it very well," she said; "but I'm sorry now that I wasn't more patient. Poor old uncle, he didn't have a very happy life."

"Well, you can't blame yourself for that. You did everything in your power to make it pleasant for him, and if he wouldn't accept your efforts, you certainly have nothing for which to reproach yourself."

"Yes, I have," she declared; "we had an awful quarrel last night, and when Uncle left me he was very angry. I hate to think of our last interview."

"The usual subject, I suppose," said young Lawrence, looking sympathetically at his cousin; "have you sent for Leroy?"

This question confirmed my fears. Mr. Lawrence had certainly implied by association of ideas, that Miss Pembroke's quarrel with her uncle the night before had had to do with Graham Leroy in some way. This might refer only to financial matters. But my jealous apprehension made me suspect a more personal side to the story.

She answered that she had sent a message to Leroy, and then again, without a moment's warning, Miss Pembroke burst into one of those convulsive fits of sobbing. I was glad Laura was still there, for she seemed able to soothe the girl as I'm sure no one else could have done.

His cousin's grief seemed to affect George Lawrence deeply, but again he endeavored to suppress any exhibition of emotion. His white face grew whiter, and he clinched his hands until the knuckles stood out like knots, but he spoke no word of sympathy or comfort.

I felt myself slightly at a loss in the presence of his repressed feeling, and as I did not think myself sufficiently acquainted with him to offer any word of sympathy, I said nothing.

It was into this somewhat difficult situation that the two doctors came. They looked exceedingly grave; indeed, their faces bore an expression of awe that seemed even beyond what the case demanded.

"Ah, George," said Doctor Masterson, grasping the hand of the young man, "I'm glad you're here. Did Janet send for you?"

"Yes, doctor; she telephoned, and I came at once. I'm indeed surprised and shocked at Uncle Robert's sudden death. Had you ever thought such a thing likely to happen?"

"No," said Doctor Masterson, and his voice had a peculiar ring, as of a man proving his own opinion.

Apparently Janet Pembroke was accustomed to the inflections of the old doctor's voice, for she looked suddenly up at him, as if he had said something more. Her crying spell was over, for the time at least, and her white face had again assumed its haughty and inscrutable expression.

"Was it heart disease?" she inquired, looking straight at Doctor Masterson.

"No," he replied; "it was not. Nor was it apoplexy, nor disease of any sort. Mr. Robert Pembroke did not die a natural death; he was killed while he slept."

I suppose to a man of Doctor Masterson's brusk, curt manner it was natural to announce this fact so baldly; but it seemed to me nothing short of brutality to fling the statement in the face of that quivering, shrinking girl.

"Killed!" she said, clasping her hands tightly. "Murdered!"

"Yes," said the doctor; "murdered in a peculiar fashion, and by a means of devilish ingenuity. Indeed, I must confess that had it not been for Doctor Post's conviction that the death was not natural, and his determination to discover the cause, it might never have been found out."

"Was he shot?" asked Janet, and it seemed to me she spoke like one in a trance.

"Shot? No!" said Doctor Masterson. "He was stabbed, or rather pierced, with a long, thin pin—a hat-pin, you know. Stabbed in the back of his neck, at the base of the brain, as he lay asleep. He never knew it. The pin broke off in the wound, and death was immediate, caused by cerebral hemorrhage. Doctor Post and I have made a most thorough examination, and we are convinced that these are the facts. Mr. Pembroke was lying on his side, in a most natural position, and was, in all probability, sleeping soundly. This gave the murderer an excellent opportunity to aim the deadly pin with careful precision, and to pierce the brain with a swift stab. The result of this was precisely the same as a sudden and fatal apoplectic stroke. Though there may have been a tremor or slight quiver of certain muscles, there was no convulsion or contortion, and Mr. Pembroke's face still retains the placid look of sleep. Death must have taken place, we conclude, at or near midnight."

We who heard this sat as if paralyzed. It was so unexpected, so fearfully sudden, so appalling, that there seemed to be no words fit to express our feelings.

Then George Lawrence spoke. "Who did it?" he said, and his

white face and compressed lips showed the struggle he was making for self-control.

"I don't know," and Doctor Masterson spoke mechanically, as if thinking of something else.

"No, of course, we don't know," broke in Doctor Post, who seemed a bit inclined to emphasize his own importance. And perhaps this was but natural, as the older doctor had plainly stated that but for Doctor Post's insistent investigation they might never have discovered the crime.

"But we must immediately set to work to find out who did this dreadful deed," Doctor Post went on; and though I felt repelled at the avidity he showed, I knew he was right. Though the others seemed partially stunned by the suddenly disclosed fact, I foresaw the dreadful experiences that must follow in its train.

Miss Pembroke, though still sitting by Laura's side, had broken away from her encircling arm. The girl sat upright, her great eyes fixed on Doctor Masterson's face. She showed no visible emotion, but seemed to be striving to realize the situation.

"Murdered!" she breathed in a low whisper; "Uncle Robert murdered!"

Then, without another word, her eyes traveled slowly round the room, resting on each person in turn. Her glance was calm, yet questioning. It almost seemed as if she suspected some one of us to be guilty of the crime. Or was it that she was seeking help and sympathy for herself? If so she could stop with me. She need look no further. I knew that in the near future she would want help, and that of a legal nature. She had herself said, or at least implied, that she would not look for such help from Graham Leroy. If this were true, and not merely a bit of feminine perversity, I vowed to myself that mine should be the helping hand outstretched to her in her hour of need.

"There is much to be done," Doctor Post continued, and his mind was so occupied with the greater facts of the situation, that he almost ignored Miss Pembroke. He addressed himself to Doctor Masterson, but it was easily seen that this was a mere form, and he himself quite evidently intended to be the real director of affairs. "We must find out who was the intruder, doubtless a professional burglar, who committed this awful deed. We must search the room for clues, and that, too, at once, before time and circumstance may obliterate them."

Although I didn't show it, I couldn't help a slight feeling of amusement at this speech. It was so palpably evident that Doctor Post possessed what he himself would doubtless call the Detective Instinct; and, moreover, it was clearly indicated that his knowledge

23

of the proper methods of procedure were gained from the best detective fiction! Not that he was wrong in his suggestion, but it was not the time, nor was it his place to investigate the hypothetical "clues."

Doctor Masterson appreciated this point, and with a slightly disapproving shake of his wise, old head, he observed: "I think those things are not in our province, Doctor Post. We have performed our duty. We have learned the method and means of Robert Pembroke's death; we have made our report, and our duties are ended. The case has passed out of our hands, and such details as clues and evidence, are in the domain of the coroner and inspector."

Doctor Post looked a little chagrined. But he quickly covered it, and effusively agreed with the older doctor.

"Quite so, quite so," he said; "I was merely suggesting, in what is perhaps an over-zealous desire to be of assistance. What you say, Doctor Masterson, is entirely true. And now," he added, again bristling with an assumption of importance, "and now, we must send for the coroner."

24

V

SEVERAL CLUES

I had often told Laura that if I ever did fall in love it would be at first sight, and now it had come. Not only Janet Pembroke's beauty and the pathetic appeal of her sorrowful face attracted me, but I was fascinated by the mystery of the girl.

The astounding news that had just been told her was so much worse than the mere fact of her uncle's death, that I fully expected her to show her emotion in desperate hysterics. But instead, it seemed to rouse in her a spirit of courage and self-reliance, and though it was quite evident that she was making a great effort, yet she ably succeeded in controlling herself perfectly.

There was no use blinking the fact; I had fallen in love with Janet Pembroke. And as the truth of the fearful tragedy penetrated her dazed brain, and she seemed so sadly in need of comfort and help my impulse was to go to her, and tell her of my sympathy and regard.

As this was out of the question, I was glad to see Laura sit by the girl's side and soothe her with kindly caresses. But, to my surprise, Janet did not faint, nor did she seem in any danger of physical collapse. On the contrary, Doctor Post's remark seemed to arouse her to action. She sat up very straight, and, though the rest of her face was perfectly white, a red spot glowed in either cheek.

"The coroner?" she said, in a strained, unnatural voice. "What would he do?"

"It is necessary, my child, that he be summoned," said Doctor Masterson, "since your uncle did not die a natural death."

"But what will he do?" persisted Janet.

"He will ask questions of all who know anything about the matter, and try to discover the one who did the awful deed."

"Of course, Janet," observed George Lawrence, "we must call the coroner. It is always done, I believe, in such a case as this."

"Very well," said Janet; "but it is all so dreadful—I can't realize it. Who killed Uncle Robert? Was it a burglar? Did he steal anything?"

She seemed to be talking quite at random. George answered her kindly, and his manner was gentle and affectionate.

"We don't know, Janet dear," he said. "That is what the coroner will inquire into."

I was thankful that my own business did not imperatively

demand my presence at my office that day, and I concluded to stay where I was, at any rate, until the coroner arrived.

I would doubtless be called as a witness, and, too, I trusted I could be of help to Janet.

The girl puzzled while she fascinated me. She seemed so helpless and alone, and yet she showed a strange courage—almost bravado.

George Lawrence, too, was reserved and self-contained, and I imagined they both inherited something of their dead uncle's strength of character.

Doctor Masterson had telephoned for the coroner, who said he would come soon and bring an inspector.

Then Laura persuaded Miss Pembroke to go with her across to our own apartment, and rest there for a time. This plan commended itself to Doctor Masterson, and he told Janet not to return until he sent for her.

Doctor Post said he would return to his office, but would come up to the apartment again when called for.

He contrived to have a short talk with me before leaving.

"There's more to this than appears on the surface," he declared, with the air of imparting information of value. "This is a most cold-blooded murder, carefully planned and cleverly carried out. The criminal is no ordinary sneak thief or burglar."

"That may be," I returned, "but if so, it is the coroner's place to discover and punish the murderer. Surely we can do nothing."

"We ought to," urged Doctor Post; "we ought to examine the whole place carefully for clues."

"I confess, Doctor Post," I returned, "that I should be glad to do so. My inclinations, like yours, are toward going to work at once. But we are not in authority, and Doctor Masterson is. It is only courteous to him and to Miss Pembroke to acquiesce in their wishes."

So, reluctantly, Doctor Post went away, and I observed that Doctor Masterson seemed relieved at his departure.

"It's a bad business," said the doctor to young Lawrence. "I can't understand it."

"It's horrible!" exclaimed George Lawrence, covering his face with his hands. "Why, I was here yesterday afternoon, and Uncle Robert was particularly well, and particularly——"

He paused, and with a grim smile Doctor Masterson completed the sentence: "Particularly cantankerous?"

"Yes, sir, he was," said Lawrence candidly. "I think I never saw him in a worse rage, and all about nothing. He stormed at Janet

26

until the poor girl cried, and then he scolded her for that. But I suppose his gout was pretty bad, and that always made him ugly."

"Where do you live now, George?" inquired Doctor Masterson.

"I've bachelor rooms down in Washington Square. Not as comfortable in some ways as I was here, but good enough on the whole. I must make a home for Janet somewhere now. It's all dreadful, to be sure, but, really, she'll be happier without Uncle Robert, in every way."

"She inherits property?" I asked, and, because of Lawrence's confidential manner, my casual question did not seem impertinent.

"She and I are the only heirs," he said straightforwardly. "Uncle Robert's will is no secret. It was made long ago, and as we are his only relatives he left us equal inheritors. I don't care about that part of it, but I'm glad Janet is to have some money of her own. Uncle Robert was mighty close with her. I made money enough for my own needs, but Janet couldn't do that, and she had to scrimp outrageously. She's so proud, she won't accept a cent from me, and between uncle's miserliness and his temper she has led an awful life."

"Then I can't feel real regret that Mr. Pembroke is gone," I said, "except that the manner of his taking off is so horrible. Do you suppose that it is the work of burglars?"

"Must have been," said Lawrence. "I haven't looked around at all—I hate all that sort of thing—but I suppose the coroner will clear up all mystery."

"Now, on the contrary," said I, "I have a liking for detective work, and, if there is any occasion for it, I'll be glad to do anything I can for you."

George Lawrence seemed not to hear me.

"Uncle Robert hadn't an enemy in the world, that I know of," he said musingly; "so it must have been a burglar or marauder of some sort."

"Very unusual method for a burglar," said I, thinking of the hat-pin. "Would you mind if I looked about a little bit? I'd like to find the other end of that pin."

"What pin?" asked Lawrence.

"The pin that killed your uncle. The doctors say it was a hat-pin, broken off close to the flesh."

"A hat-pin? How awful!"

The young man gave a shudder, as if sensitive to gruesome pictures.

"Yes," I went on; "and if we could find the head end that broke off, it might be a clue to the murderer."

"Oh, yes, I see. Well, certainly, go and look about all you

27

choose. But excuse me from that sort of thing. I'll get the best detectives, if necessary, but I can't do anything in that way myself."

I readily understood this attitude in one so closely related to the victim of the dreadful deed, and at his permission I determined to search the whole apartment thoroughly. We had been alone during this conversation, as Doctor Masterson had returned to his late patient's room, and the servant, Charlotte, had not reappeared.

I went directly to Mr. Pembroke's bedroom, but when there, I hesitated for a moment before addressing Doctor Masterson.

And then he spoke first; "I freely confess," he said, "that I owe to Doctor Post the discovery of the truth. I was positive it was not a natural death, but my old eyes failed to detect that tiny speck that gave us the solution. However, that does not give Doctor Post the right to pry into the affairs of the Pembroke household. It is now a case for the Coroner, and no one else has a right to interfere."

"I appreciate your attitude, Doctor Masterson," I returned, "but Mr. Lawrence, who is, of course, in authority, has given me permission to search this room, and in fact the whole apartment, for possible clues that may help to solve the mystery."

"Humph," grunted the old Doctor, peering at me through his glasses; "if George says so, of course you may do what you like, but I warn you you'd better let the matter alone."

"Have you any suspicions?" I asked suddenly.

"Suspicions? Goodness, no! How could I have any suspicions? You must be crazy!" And without another word the old man hurriedly left the room.

After this exhibition of anger on his part, I felt myself in an unpleasant position. Perhaps I had been over-zealous in my desire to be of service to Miss Pembroke. Perhaps there were clues or evidences better left undiscovered. But, pshaw! such ideas were absurd. Robert Pembroke had been murdered. It was the duty of any American citizen to do anything in his power toward the discovery of the criminal.

Convinced of this, I set to work at once to make a thorough search of the room for anything that might seem indicative.

I merely glanced at the quiet figure lying on the bed, for such evidence as that might show must be determined by the coroner's physicians. I was only seeking stray clues that might otherwise be overlooked, and that might prove to be of value.

Seating myself in front of the open desk, I noted the carefully filed and labeled documents that filled its pigeon-holes.

I could not bring myself to look into these; for though Lawrence had given me unlimited permission, I felt that this personal sort of investigation should be made only by a member of the family.

But in plain view lay a rubber band and a pencilled memorandum which appeared to have been hastily thrown down. The paper slip seemed to show a receipt for ten thousand dollars brought to Robert Pembroke in payment for some stock sold by his brokers. This might all be an unimportant business detail, but in view of the otherwise tidy condition of the desk, it seemed to me to indicate that the intruder had stolen the money or security noted on the slip, leaving the paper and rubber band behind him.

I might be over-fanciful, but there was certainly no harm in preserving this possible evidence, and I put the slip of paper and the rubber band in my pocket-book.

I saw nothing further of interest about the desk, and I turned my attention to the waste basket. On top of a few other torn papers lay the two stubs of theater tickets, which I had myself thrown there, before I knew that there was a crime in question.

I transferred the two bits of paper to my pocket-book and proceeded to investigate further the torn papers in the basket. They seemed to me to have no bearing whatever upon the case, being mostly circulars, receipted small bills, or ordinary business notes.

However, toward the bottom, I found a torn telegram, which pieced together read, "Expect me on Wednesday evening."

It was addressed to Robert Pembroke, and it was signed J. S.

Of course I put this away with my other findings, for though it might be of no importance whatever, yet the contrary might be equally true.

Rising from the desk, I saw a folded paper on the floor near by and picked it up. This proved to be a time-table of local trains on the Lackawanna Railroad. It was not probable that the burglar had left this as a clue to his travels,—it was more likely that it had belonged to Mr. Pembroke or his niece,—but I put it in my pocket, with the general idea of collecting any evidence possible.

Further minute search of the floor revealed nothing whatever but an ordinary hair-pin. With two women in the household, this was not an astonishing find, but I kept it, among my other acquisitions.

At last, feeling convinced that there was nothing more to be learned from the room, I was about to leave it, when I paused by the bedside. Near the foot of the bed, and outside the counterpane, I noticed a handkerchief. I picked it up and its large size proved it to belong to a man. Though slightly crumpled, it was quite fresh, and in the corner three small letters, W. S. G. were embroidered in fine white stitches. These initials were not Robert Pembroke's, and there were of course many plausible explanations of the presence of the handkerchief. But since it didn't seem to represent the property of

29

any member of the household, I felt myself justified in folding it carefully and putting it in my pocket.

As I left the room I cast a final glance around it, feeling certain that a more skilled detective would have discovered many things that I had overlooked, and probably would have scorned to look upon as clues the collection of articles I had pocketed.

But knowing nothing of the personality or habits of Robert Pembroke, it was difficult indeed to judge intelligently the contents and condition of his bedroom.

VI

THE INQUEST BEGINS

When I returned to the drawing-room, I found the coroner had already arrived, accompanied by Inspector Crawford.

Mr. Ross, the coroner, looked like a capable, active man, while Mr. Crawford's face wore the blank and inscrutable expression which is supposed to be part of the detective's stock in trade. I have often wondered whether this imperturbability is not used quite as often to cloak utter ignorance as to hide secret knowledge.

They had been in the house but a few moments, and Doctor Masterson was making them acquainted with the main facts of the case. Young Lawrence was assisting in the recital, but whether because of his natural disinclination for gruesome subjects, or because of his relationship with the dead man, he seemed unwilling to talk, and referred all questions to Doctor Masterson.

I took a seat, and remained a mere listener; as I knew it was not yet the time to tell of any discoveries I might have made.

But beyond a brief introduction by the aged doctor and a brief acknowledgment of it by the coroner, little attention was paid to me, and I listened with interest to Mr. Ross's pertinent questions and quick decisions.

Being possessed of the facts of the case, and having learned all that those present could tell him, the Coroner determined to hold a preliminary inquest right then and there.

Although as a lawyer I have had more or less experience in these matters it seemed to me an incredibly short space of time before a jury was impanelled and the examination of witnesses begun.

There were but a half-dozen men on the jury, and these seemed to spring up out of the very ground. As a matter of fact, Inspector Crawford had gone out and brought some back with him, and others were summoned by telephone.

A reporter also had materialized from somewhere, and was sharpening his pencils in a business-like way as he sat at a small table.

The whole assembly had an official effect, and it seemed as if the magic of some evil fairy had transformed the luxurious drawing-room into a Hall of Justice.

George Lawrence was sent across to bring Miss Pembroke back, and when they came Laura accompanied them.

31

Doctor Masterson was called as the first witness.

He testified as to the manner and cause of Mr. Pembroke's death.

"Were you Mr. Pembroke's physician?" asked the coroner.

"Yes; I have attended him for twenty years."

"He had no ailments or symptoms that would make his sudden death probable?"

"None that I know of."

"Yet you thought at first that he died of apoplexy?"

"I did, because it seemed to be a case of cerebral hemorrhage, and I looked only for natural causes."

"Why did you call Doctor Post?"

"I didn't feel satisfied to trust my uncorroborated opinion, and desired the advice of another physician."

"After you learned beyond all doubt that Mr. Pembroke had been wilfully murdered, did you observe anything that might point toward a possible criminal?"

"No, nothing at all. I found a key in the bed, which had doubtless slipped from under the pillow. It seemed to be an especial key, as of a box or drawer."

"Where is the key?"

"I handed it to Mr. Landon for safe keeping."

At the request of the Coroner I produced the key, and gave it to him. He turned to Miss Pembroke.

"Was this key the property of your uncle?" he asked.

"I don't know," she replied; "it may have been."

"You have never seen it before, then?"

"Not to my knowledge. But my uncle has several boxes in the bank and in the safe deposit company, and it may belong to one of them."

"Do you know anything of this key, Mr. Lawrence?" pursued the Coroner, turning to the young man.

"I know nothing whatever of my uncle's business affairs, or his boxes or keys. Doubtless his lawyer could tell you of these matters."

"Who is his lawyer, and why has he not been summoned?" said Mr. Ross. He looked at Miss Pembroke, as if she were the one in authority.

"We have sent for him," replied Miss Pembroke, "but he is out of town." As she spoke, the girl's cheeks flushed to a delicate pink, and my heart sank as I began to fear that she was deeply interested in the handsome lawyer, and that her apparently adverse remarks concerning him had been prompted by feminine pique.

The Coroner laid the key on the table before him, as if

postponing its further consideration and then called Doctor Post as a witness.

The young man, who had been again summoned from his office, gave his testimony in a fussy, self-important sort of way.

His evidence agreed with all Doctor Masterson had said, and continued thus:

"I felt, like Doctor Masterson, that the effects were not quite those of apoplexy, and so made a thorough examination for other causes of death. At the base of the brain I discovered a small black speck. It proved to be the end of a long pin, which was so deeply imbedded as to be almost invisible. It is not strange that Doctor Masterson should not have discovered it, as it was completely covered by the long, thick white hair of the head."

"This pin, you say, is a hat-pin?"

"A part of a hat-pin. It was evidently inserted while the victim was asleep. It was then, either intentionally or accidentally, broken in half. Owing to a peculiar tendency of human flesh, the pin was probably drawn in a trifle deeper than when left there by the criminal's hand, and thus almost disappeared from view."

"And it was this stab of a pin that caused death?"

"Undoubtedly—and immediately."

Except for a few technical points regarding the cause and effect of cerebral hemorrhage, that was the gist of Doctor Post's evidence.

As the case was indisputably a murder, there being no possibility of suicide, the next thing was to discover the criminal.

Coroner Ross went about his work in a most methodical and systematic manner. His witnesses were called, sworn, questioned, and dismissed with a despatch that amazed me.

The agent of The Hammersleigh, who also lived in the house, was examined next.

"Your name?" asked the Coroner.

"James Whitaker."

"Your occupation?"

"I am agent and superintendent of The Hammersleigh. I live in an apartment on the first floor."

"How long have you had Robert Pembroke as a tenant?"

"Mr. Pembroke has occupied this apartment for three years."

"Of how many members did the family consist?"

"Until about three months ago, there were three in the family. Mr. Pembroke, his niece and nephew. Also, one servant was kept, usually a colored woman. About three months ago, the nephew, Mr. Lawrence, moved away."

"They have proved satisfactory as tenants?"

33

"Exceedingly so, with one exception. It was always difficult to collect from Mr. Pembroke the money due for his rent."

"He was not a poor man?"

"Quite the contrary. He was a very wealthy man, but he hated to part with his money."

"When did you see him last?"

"Yesterday afternoon. About two o'clock I came up here to ask him for his rent which was overdue."

"He paid you?"

"Yes; he paid me with bills of large denomination, taken from a very large roll of similar bills. He must have had about ten thousand dollars in the roll."

I listened with great interest to this evidence. Surely that roll of bills which Mr. Whitaker saw was the money noted on the memorandum I had found.

"Were the bills in a rubber band, and was a slip of paper with them?" I asked, for the inquest was conducted informally, and anyone spoke who chose.

"Yes," replied Whitaker, looking at me with a glance that savored of suspicion; "how did you know?"

I resented his manner, and then I suddenly remembered that I was but a new tenant, and the agent was justified in his desire to question me.

"Mr. Landon will be examined later," said the Coroner, with his authoritative air; "we will continue with the present witness. What can you say, Mr. Whitaker, of the general character of Mr. Pembroke?"

"I know little of him. As a tenant he made me no trouble at all. He never complained to me of the apartment, the management or the service. As a business man, I have no reason to think him other than upright and honorable. Further than this I had no acquaintance with him. He was not a man to invite acquaintance."

"He was of uncertain temper, I understand."

"Well, it could hardly be called uncertain." Mr. Whitaker smiled a little. "On the contrary, his temper was certain to be bad. He was an inveterate scold, and sometimes would fly into a most ungovernable rage over nothing at all. But this was not my affair; he always paid his rent,—though only under protest, and after numerous requests."

"When you saw him yesterday, was he ill-tempered?"

"Very much so. I would say unusually so, except that he was usually as cross as any man could be."

"What was he cross about?"

"Everything and nothing. He railed at the government, the

34

weather, his lawyer, his niece,—and in fact, spoke angrily upon any subject that was mentioned between us."

"Then you can tell us nothing, Mr. Whitaker, that will throw any light upon the crime that has been committed in your house?"

"Nothing at all."

"Would it be possible for a marauder or intruder to get in during the night?"

"Into the house, yes. The front doors are open until midnight. Each tenant is supposed to safeguard his own apartment."

"And you know of no questionable person who entered the house last night?"

"Certainly not. I have no reason to notice those who come or go. The elevator boy might tell you."

Mr. Whitaker was dismissed, and the elevator boy was sent for. He was rather a clever-looking young fellow of about seventeen, and his face, though impudent, was shrewd and intelligent.

"Samuel McGuire, me name is," he announced, in response to the Coroner's question; "but the fellers call me Solomon, cos I know mor'n they do. I studies and reads every chance I gets, and they jes' loafs 'round."

"Well, Samuel, what can you tell us of Mr. Pembroke?"

"Nuttin good. But then they ain't much to tell. He never trun himself loose outen his own door; but I didn't mind his bein' canned, cos I knew he couldn't pry himself loose from a tip, any way. So I never seen him since the day he came; but gee, I've often heard him! Say, the Mauretoonia's fog-horn ain't got nothin' on him! Tain't no silent treatment he gives that niece of his'n! Nur that classy brunette soivant, neither!"

"He was not even kindly-spoken to his niece, then?"

"I guess no! Gee, the foist time I seen that skoit, I t'ought I'd been shot in the eye wit' a magazine cover! An' she's as daisy actin' as she is lookin'. I sure admire Miss Pembroke!"

This was not the kind of information Mr. Ross wanted, but young McGuire rolled it forth so rapidly, and with such graphic facial expression that his audience listened, uninterrupting.

"That's enough, McGuire," said Mr. Ross, sternly; "please confine your speech to simple and direct answers to my questions."

"Sure," agreed the boy, grinning. "But I thought you wanted me to tell you all what I was wise to of the family's doin's."

"What I want to know especially, is, whether any one came into the house last evening, or late last night, who was a stranger to you?"

"Well, no; I ain't seen no Rube divin' into my cage, wot looks suspiciony. But then, you see, Mr. Coroner, I ain't on the night

35

shift. This week I goes off at six P. M. and toddles myself off to a tremblin' scenery show."

"Then you're not the elevator boy we want, at all," said Mr. Ross, greatly annoyed at this loss of time.

"Be-lieve me, I ain't! But I'm glad to add it against brother Pembroke. He never left his rooms, but, gee! he didn't have to, fer me to hear him bally-hooin'! Every time I passed this floor, 'most, he wuz a handin' it out to the young lady good an' plenty!"

McGuire was excused, and being loath to leave the room, he was materially assisted by Inspector Crawford.

Though not an attractive specimen of his class, and though his evidence was unimportant, he had at least helped to prove the irascibility of the late Mr. Pembroke, and the fact that his ugly temper was often vented upon his niece.

As I learned all this, I felt more than ever glad that Janet was at last freed from this tyrant. Indeed, my attention was only half given to the business in hand. My thoughts continually wandered to the girl who had, all unconsciously, twined herself around my heart. I found myself wondering where she would go when this was all over; how soon I could cultivate her acquaintance; and if—in the future—I could at last win her for my own. It was my first infatuation with any woman, and I gave myself up to it unreservedly, while my soul thrilled with hopes of what might some time be. To be sure, Miss Pembroke had not so much as glanced at me with other than the most formal politeness, such as she might show to any new acquaintance. But I would not let this discourage me. Because it was love at first sight on my side was no reason why it should be on hers, so I only determined to win her, if possible, and to be careful that she should not yet discover my feelings toward herself.

From these rose-colored dreams I was suddenly recalled to the dreadful realities of the occasion by hearing myself summoned as a witness.

I took the stand, hoping that some chance word or tone of my otherwise unimportant evidence might at least convince Miss Pembroke of my friendly interest in her and her affairs.

36

VII

I GIVE EVIDENCE

"Your name," said the Coroner to me.

"Otis Landon."

"You live in this house?"

"Yes, I live in the apartment across the hall, on this same floor. It is a duplicate of this apartment."

"Please tell in your own words," said Mr. Ross, "exactly what you know of this matter."

And so I told my story. "I am a lawyer, and a bachelor," I said. "My widowed sister, Mrs. Mulford, keeps house for me. As we sat at breakfast this morning the door-bell rang. Knowing from the hour—just about eight o'clock—that it was probably the hall boy with the mail, I opened the door myself, and took the letters from him. As I stood a moment, carelessly running over the mail, the boy pressed the button at the opposite apartment—the one where we now are. The colored servant came to the door, and though she unlatched it at once, it was held by a chain."

Just here Inspector Crawford interrupted me.

"The night-chain was on, you say?"

"Yes," I answered; "I heard the colored woman's voice exclaiming that she always forgot to remove the night-chain before opening the door; so she reclosed the door, unfastened the chain, and opened the door again. She then took the letters and went back to the apartment. I returned to my own breakfast. Perhaps half an hour later I started for my office. As I was waiting for the elevator to come up, my sister stood with me, chatting. When the elevator did arrive I saw a gentleman in it, who, I have since learned, is Doctor Masterson. As the car reached our floor Miss Pembroke rushed from her own apartment to meet the doctor, exclaiming that her uncle was ill. My sister and I were much concerned, and offered our assistance. A few moments later Doctor Masterson came and asked us to come over here, as Mr. Pembroke was dead and Miss Pembroke had fainted. We came at once, and have endeavored to do anything we could to help."

For some reason, Doctor Masterson seemed disturbed at my remarks. Why, I could not guess, for I had told the exact truth, and it seemed to me to have little bearing on the circumstances of the old man's death. On the other hand, what I had said seemed to give satisfaction to the Coroner. He nodded his head affirmatively several times, and it was plain to be seen that my testimony corroborated, at least did not contradict some already formed theory of his own.

After a slight pause, while he seemed to weigh in his mind the evidence I had given, he resumed his questioning.

"I am told Mr. Landon, that you searched Mr. Pembroke's bedroom for possible clues. Did you find any?"

"I am not sure," I replied; "in a room that one has never seen before, it is difficult to know what belongs there and what does not. However I picked up a few articles, which, though they may be informative, are equally likely to be of no importance to us in our search."

I offered first in evidence the memorandum of money and the rubber band still around it. The slight crumpling of the paper, seemed to show a hasty removal of the money,—if money had been enclosed.

"This seems to me to be of decided importance," commented Mr. Ross; "indeed, unless some member of the household can throw light on the matter, I shall conclude that a sum of money was stolen from Mr. Pembroke, and that the robbery constituted the motive for either previous or subsequent murder."

This seemed to me both rational and logical, and I waited with interest the next questions.

Mr. Ross first addressed Miss Pembroke.

"Do you know anything concerning this money?" he inquired, simply.

Janet Pembroke was sitting on a sofa, next to Laura. As, with the exception of the colored servant, they were the only women present, Laura assumed the attitude of chaperon and protector to the young girl. And it was doubtless due to my sister's sympathy and support, that Miss Pembroke was preserving a calm demeanor. But at the Coroner's question, she became greatly agitated. She trembled, and her fingers grasped nervously at Laura's arm as she stammered a reply.

"I—I—I know that Uncle Robert had a large sum of money in his possession yesterday."

"Where did he get it?"

"His lawyer, Mr. Leroy, brought it to him night before last."

"Was it as much as ten thousand dollars, as this memorandum seems to indicate?"

"I—I—I think it was."

What was the matter with the girl? If she had stolen the money herself, she could not have acted more guiltily embarrassed. To me, the idea of theft in connection with Janet Pembroke was absurd, but

38

I could readily see from the countenances of the men about me, that the situation impressed them quite otherwise.

"Was Mr. Pembroke in the habit of keeping such large sums of money in the house?"

"No; it was most unusual."

"How, then, did it happen in this instance?"

"I am not quite sure;" and now Miss Pembroke looked anxious and puzzled, rather than frightened, as she had appeared before, "I think he expected a man to come to see him, to whom he would pay the money."

"Do you know the name of this man?"

"It was,—no,—I do not."

I think no one present believed this statement. It was made with too much hesitation and uncertainty.

"Are you sure, Miss Pembroke that you do not know the name of the man for whom your uncle intended the money?"

The girl's uncertainty appeared to vanish. "I do not!" she cried; "my uncle was not in the habit of confiding to me his business matters. But he often spoke in loud tones, and quite unintentionally I overheard a few words between him and Mr. Leroy, which gave me the impression that he intended the money for some man who would soon call to receive it."

"Do you know anything concerning this money?" Mr. Ross then said, addressing his question to George Lawrence.

The young man had been sitting watching his cousin in silence. He seemed absorbed in deep thought and roused himself suddenly as the Coroner spoke to him.

"No," he said, with an air of detachment from the whole affair; "I know nothing at all of these matters. I saw my uncle for a few moments yesterday afternoon, but he said nothing to me about money, or his financial affairs of any sort."

"Did you see your uncle in his own room?" I asked, of Mr. Lawrence.

"Yes," he replied giving me a glance, which, though coldly polite, seemed to resent my interference. But I was not to be baffled in my intent.

"Was his desk open when you were there?" I went on.

"I didn't notice definitely, but it is usually open. Indeed, I think I have never seen it closed."

"And did you see a large roll of bills in it?" I relentlessly pursued.

"I did not; nor should I have remarked it if I had. If my uncle chose to be careless with his cash it was not my affair."

"It is possible the money may yet be found," observed the

39

coroner; "Mr. Pembroke may have put it away more safely. Search must be made for it, but at present we will continue our verbal evidence. Mr. Landon, what else did you find in your search?"

"I found this time-table," I replied, feeling a little foolish as I gave it to the Coroner.

"H'm, local trains on the Lackawanna," he murmured, as he glanced at it; "Miss Pembroke, is this likely to have belonged to your uncle?"

Again the girl became agitated. "I think not," she said; "no, it couldn't have been his. Uncle Robert never went out anywhere. Why should he have a time-table?"

"Is it your own?"

"No; I have not travelled on that road for a long time, and have had no thought of doing so."

Then the Coroner turned to Charlotte. "Do you know anything about this?" he asked; "have you ever seen it before?"

"Laws, no!" replied the colored woman, rolling her eyes distractedly. "I nebber trabbels myself, and Marse Pembroke, he nebber trabbled outside de do'. And Miss Janet she ain't nebber been trabblin' since I'se been here—dat I knows on."

"Then it would seem," said Mr. Ross, "that this time-table must have been left in the room by some outsider. Do you know anything of it, Mr. Lawrence?"

"No; I rarely use time-tables. But it does not seem to me important. Leroy may have left it, he's always travelling about."

Immediately the time-table seemed to shrink into insignificance, and the Coroner tossed it aside and asked to see my next exhibit.

A little chagrined at the apparent unimportance of my clues, I produced the handkerchief.

"This lay on the foot of the bed," I said; "I noticed it only because it bears initials which are not those of Mr. Pembroke."

"W. S. G.," read the Coroner as he examined the corner of the handkerchief. "Do you recognize those initials, Miss Pembroke?"

"No;" and the girl's face this time expressed mere blank amazement; "I know of no one with those initials. It is a man's handkerchief?"

"Yes," replied the Coroner, holding up to view the large square of linen; "And it is of fine texture and dainty finish."

"And beautifully hand-embroidered," said Miss Pembroke, as she rose from her seat and took the handkerchief in her hand.

She seemed in a quite different mood now. Apparently the handkerchief had roused her curiosity. She turned to Charlotte with it, saying, "You've never seen this before, have you, Charlotte?"

"No, Miss Janet; I nebber seed dat hank'chif befo'. Dat's sure! It ain't Marse Pembroke's, nor it aint's Master George's, and dat's all de men dey is in dis fambly."

"It couldn't have been left by Mr. Leroy," went on Miss Pembroke, musingly; "I cannot explain it. It's a mystery to me."

She returned the handkerchief to the Coroner, and resumed her seat beside Laura.

"It would seem," said Mr. Ross, "that whoever left this handkerchief in Mr. Pembroke's room, was a man of refined tastes,—but we must defer definite assumption of that sort until after further inquiry. You have something else to show us, Mr. Landon?"

Without a word I handed him the two stubs of theatre tickets.

"National Theatre," he read. "Your uncle never went to the theatre, Miss Pembroke?" he inquired.

"Never," she answered, quietly.

"You sometimes go yourself?"

"Occasionally, yes. But I know nothing of those tickets. I have never been to the National Theatre."

I was glad to hear this, for the National Theatre, though entirely reputable, was of the Music Hall class, and it pleased me that Janet Pembroke did not incline to that type of entertainment.

In response to inquiries, Charlotte asserted volubly, and George Lawrence haughtily, that they knew nothing of these mysterious bits of pasteboard. The only inference was, then, that they had been dropped in Mr. Pembroke's room by some one who was calling on him recently.

And then, as a final offering to the mysterious accumulation of evidence, I handed to the Coroner the torn telegram I had found in the waste basket. It had been torn across but once, and was easily pieced together. The Coroner read it aloud:

"Expect me on Wednesday evening. Signed, J. S. Sent from East Lynnwood, New Jersey. H'm, that links it to the Lackawanna time-table, as East Lynnwood is on a branch of that road."

"Are you sure of that?" asked George Lawrence.

"No, I'm not sure," returned Mr. Ross; "but it's my impression that East Lynnwood is off that way, somewhere."

"I'm not sure, myself," said Lawrence, and no one present seemed to know where East Lynnwood was, and the time-table was only for stations on the main line, not to branches. I determined to look it up for myself as soon as the inquest was over, for surely these hints I had picked up must lead somewhere.

41

"Do you know who J. S. may be?" the Coroner asked of Miss Pembroke.

"No," she replied, briefly, but again I had a conviction that she was not speaking truthfully. The very vehemence with which she spoke seemed to me to betoken a desperate intention to hide the truth, but of this I could not be sure.

"But if your Uncle received a telegram, bidding him expect a caller last evening, would you not be likely to know about it?"

"Not necessarily," returned Miss Pembroke; "My Uncle never informed me of his business appointments or arrangements. But no one did call upon him last evening, of that I'm certain."

"The telegram may have been a blind," said one of the jurors, wagging his head sagaciously. He seemed to think he had said something exceedingly clever, but Coroner Ross paid no heed to him. Indeed the Coroner seemed to care little about material clues, and was anxious to continue his verbal inquiries.

After a few more questions, of no definite importance, I was excused, and my sister Laura was called to the stand.

Her evidence regarding the occurrences which led to our introduction on the scene, was practically an echo of my own, and consequently not of direct importance. The Coroner endeavored to learn from her something concerning the unpleasant relations between Mr. Pembroke and his niece, but though Laura had expressed herself often and frankly to me on the subject, she would say nothing in public concerning it. She declared that she was totally unacquainted with the Pembrokes, and had never spoken to Miss Janet until that morning, and had never been in their apartment before.

Of course she was soon excused, and next Charlotte, the colored servant, was called.

She responded in a state of terrified excitement. She was nervously loquacious, and Mr. Ross was obliged to command her to answer his questions as shortly as possible, and not dilate on them or express any opinions.

"At what hour did you rise?"

"'Bout seben, sah."

"Did you then prepare breakfast?"

"Yes, sah—bacon 'n' eggs, an' cereal, an'——"

"Never mind what the meal consisted of. Did you see any one before you served breakfast?"

"Only the hall boy, when I went to take the lettahs, sah."

"He rang the bell?"

"Yes, sah. He allus does. An' I dun gib de do' a yank, but dat ol' chain held it. I 'clar to goodness, I can't nebber 'member dat chain."

"Have you been with this household long?"

"I's been here six weeks, sah. But I was gwine to leave, any way. I couldn't stan' de way Mr. Pembroke called me names, sah. Miss Janet she's mighty nice lady, but de ol' massa he was too much fo' anybody."

VIII

AN AWFUL IMPLICATION

"Never mind your opinions of your employers," commanded the coroner sternly. "Simply answer my questions. What did you do with the letters?"

"I took 'em to Miss Janet."

"Is that your custom?"

"Yes, sah. She looks 'em ober, an' if dey's bills she doesn't gib 'em to Mr. Pembroke till after breakfast, sah."

"Where was Miss Pembroke when you gave her the mail?"

"In her own room, sah, jes' finishin' dressin'."

"What did you do next?"

"Den Miss Janet she tole me to knock on Mr. Pembroke's door, so he'd know breakfas' was ready. An' I did, but he didn't answer. Gen'ally he hollers at me when I knock. So I knock again an' again, an' when he don't holler out cross-like, I 'mos' know sumpin's wrong. So I went and tol' Miss Janet dat her uncle didn't answer back. An' she say: 'Oh, pshaw, he's asleep. Knock again.'"

"Did you do so?"

"Yes, sah. An' still he don't holler out ugly, like he always do. Den I got awful scart, an' I begged Miss Janet to go in his room. An' den she did. An' she scream out: 'Oh, Charlotte, uncle has had a stroke or sumpin! What shall we do?' An' I say: 'Oh, Miss Janet, send for de doctor.' An' she telephoned right away, an' bimeby he come."

"That will do," said Mr. Ross. "From that time on, we have had the history of events. But to go back to last night. Were you in the house last evening?"

"Yes, sah; dat is, I was, after nine o'clock. I went out befo' dat, but I come in sharp at nine, as Miss Janet had tole me to."

"There were no guests here when you returned?"

"No sah; no comp'ny. Miss Janet and her uncle—dey sat in de drawin' room, conversationin'."

The way Charlotte's eyes rolled about, and the quizzical look on her face, gave a distinct hint as to the nature of the conversation.

"Was the conversation of a pleasant sort?" the Coroner could not refrain from saying.

"Laws, no, sah! Marse Pembroke, he nebber conversed pleasantly, sah. He jes' nachelly scold Miss Janet always. Sometimes wusser dan odders,—but always scoldin'."

44

"What was he scolding her about?"

"I dunno. I jes' walked by de do', but I 'spect,——" Here Charlotte rolled her eyes toward Miss Pembroke, and the expression on that young lady's face, was so unmistakably a desire for Charlotte to cease her revelations, that I was not surprised at the colored woman's obedience to it.

"Go on," said Mr. Ross, "what do you suspect?"

"Nuffin, sah! nuffin 'tall."

"But you were about to say something?"

Again Charlotte rolled her eyes toward Miss Pembroke, and again the girl gave her a look which as plainly as words, forbade her to continue.

"Oh, laws," said Charlotte, easily, "den I 'spect old Marse Pembroke wuz jes' blowin' her up kase de bills wuz so big. He always said de bills wuz 'normous, even if dey wuz as small as anything. Dey wasn't no pleasin' dat man, no how."

Mr. Ross abandoned this line of query and began a fresh subject.

"Sit here," he said to Charlotte, indicating a seat where she could not see Miss Pembroke, who was directly behind her. "Now," he went on, "remember you are under oath to tell the truth, and see that you do it! Did you hear Mr. Pembroke or Miss Pembroke make any reference to a large sum of money?"

Charlotte said nothing. She twisted and turned in an endeavor to look round at Miss Pembroke, but the Coroner sternly ordered her to sit still and to answer the question. He added some remarks of a warning nature about punishment for untruthfulness, which so worked upon her half-ignorant mind that Charlotte became greatly agitated.

"Mus' I tell de trufe to you-all?" she gasped, in a stage whisper.

"Yes, and quickly," commanded Mr. Ross.

"Well, den, Miss Janet, she did ask Mr. Pembroke for a lot o' money."

"And he refused her?"

"Well, sah, he 'llowed as he'd gib it to her, ef she'd marry dat Leroy man."

At this point George Lawrence interposed.

"I cannot think it necessary," he said, "to allow the exposure of these personal matters, and especially through the medium of an ignorant servant."

I quite agreed with the speaker, and I admired the manly, dignified manner which accompanied his words. It seemed to me distinctly mean and petty to wrest these intimate revelations from the colored woman.

45

"In a case like this, Mr. Lawrence," the Coroner replied, "the law is justified in getting evidence from any reliable source. And I am convinced that this woman is telling us the truth."

"But truths that are irrelevant to the matter in hand," declared Lawrence. "Your investigation, I take it, is for the purpose of discovering the murderer of Mr. Robert Pembroke; and it surely cannot aid you to pry into the personal affairs of Miss Pembroke."

"It is quite possible," said the Coroner, coldly, "that Miss Pembroke's personal affairs may have some bearing on our quest. However I agree with you, to this extent. I think it will be preferable not to learn of these matters through the testimony of a menial. I think I should prefer to learn the truth from Miss Pembroke herself. Miss Pembroke, will you now give your evidence?"

Doctor Masterson's expression had grown even more worried than before. He seemed to me to look positively alarmed, and I wondered what it was that troubled him so.

Miss Pembroke, on the contrary, was absolutely composed, and had again assumed that air of hauteur which I had sometimes noticed on her face when I had met her before I was privileged to speak to her, but which had been utterly absent since her uncle's death.

The coroner looked at her, not unkindly, but with an air of coldness which quite matched her own.

"Your name?" he said briefly.

"Janet Pembroke."

"Your relation to the deceased?"

"That of great-niece. Robert Pembroke was my grandfather's brother."

"You lived with him?"

"I have lived with him since I was sixteen."

"Was he kind to you?"

"No."

This was said without a trace of anger or resentment, but merely in the tones of one stating a simple fact.

"Why was he not kind to you?"

"I know of no reason, save that he was not of a kindly disposition. He had a dreadful and ungovernable temper, which was doubtless due in part, at least, to the fact that he suffered greatly from gout."

"Was he—was he cruel to you?"

"Yes."

"Did he ever offer you personal violence?"

"He has struck me several times."

46

My blood boiled at these revelations. To think of that exquisite creature at the mercy of an angry brute!

"Why did you not leave him?"

"I had no other home, and, too, he needed me to look after him."

"He could afford to hire caretakers."

"Yes, but he was my only living relative, except my cousin, Mr. Lawrence, and I felt that I owed him care and attention in return for what he had always done for me. Besides, it was difficult for him to keep servants of any sort. They always left after a few of his violent exhibitions of temper."

"Was he liberal with you in money matters?"

"He was not."

"Do you refer to money for household expenses or for your personal use?"

"To both."

"Do you know the contents of your uncle's will?"

"I do."

"You know, then, that by his death you will inherit a large sum of money?"

"Yes."

This conversation was listened to intently by all present, and it seemed to me that at this point the coroner's face took on an even harder and colder look than it had had before. I wondered why he seemed so devoid of sympathy or even of common humanity as his metallic voice rang out the questions.

"You heard the testimony of Charlotte, your servant?"

"Yes."

"You corroborate it?"

"I do, so far as it concerns my actions."

"Then you saw your uncle first this morning, when Charlotte called you to his room?"

"Yes."

"And you thought him ill?"

"I feared he was dead, he looked so white and still. But I thought it might be a paralytic stroke, or something that would cause an appearance similar to that of death."

"Did you touch the body?"

"No." Miss Pembroke gave a slight shudder, which seemed to be not without its effect on the coroner.

"Why not?"

At this she looked extremely white and her lip quivered slightly, but with a sudden accession of extreme dignity she drew herself up proudly and answered:

47

"I saw no occasion to do so, and I deemed the proper thing was to send at once for our family physician."

Still the coroner eyed her in a peculiar way, I thought, as, without cessation, he continued to question her.

"When did you last see your uncle alive?"

"When he left the drawing-room last evening, to retire to his bedroom."

"Was he apparently as well as usual?"

"Quite so. His gout was troublesome, but he had no other ailment that I know of."

"At what hour was this?"

"About ten o'clock."

"Was your uncle in a bad temper when he left you?"

"He was."

"Especially so?"

"Yes."

"What was the reason?"

"He had been looking over the household accounts, and he accused me of extravagance."

"Did he often do this?"

"Invariably, upon looking over the bills."

"You always expected it, then?"

"Always," and Miss Pembroke's face showed an expression of resignation, that made it pathetic to look upon. What that poor little girl must have suffered from that parsimonious old man!

"Did your Uncle show anger with you for any other cause?"

Miss Pembroke hesitated. And then, though with a rising color in her pale face, she replied, "He did."

"I'm sorry, Miss Pembroke, to be unpleasantly inquisitive, but it is imperative that I should know the facts of the case. What was the reason of your uncle's anger, aside from the question of your household bills?"

"He was angry with me because I refused to become engaged to Mr. Leroy."

"Mr. Graham Leroy, your uncle's lawyer?"

"Yes, that is the man."

"Your uncle wished you to marry him?"

"He did."

"Mr. Leroy has asked you to become his wife?"

"He has."

The cold, even tones of the two speakers, and the quiet expressionless faces seemed to rob this strange conversation of all hint of personality. For myself, I felt a glad thrill that Janet

Pembroke could speak thus dispassionately of the man with whom I had feared she was in love. And, yet, in love with him she might be, for as a lawyer, I knew much of the vagaries and contradictions of woman's perversity; and I realized that the mere fact of Miss Pembroke's excessive calm might mean only a hiding of excessive emotion.

Inexorably the Coroner went on.

"Did your uncle promise you a large sum of money if you would marry Mr. Leroy?"

Miss Pembroke flashed a reproachful glance at Charlotte, who had of course brought about this question, but she answered, in a steady voice: "It was not of the nature of a bargain, as your words seem to imply."

"But you had asked him for a large sum of money?"

"I had done so."

"You asked him last evening?"

"Yes."

"Knowing that he had a large sum of money in the house?"

"I——I was not sure that he had." It was the first time that the girl had stammered or hesitated in her speech, and though it told against her in the minds of the jurors, yet to me it only showed a giving way of her enforced calm.

"What did you want the money for?" said the Coroner, suddenly.

Miss Pembroke looked at him, and now, her eyes flashed like those of an accusing goddess. "You have no right to ask that!" she exclaimed, "and I refuse to tell."

"It certainly has no bearing on the case," said George Lawrence, and his haughty, disdainful tones seemed like a sneer at the way the Coroner was conducting matters.

Mr. Ross turned red, but he did not repeat his question. Instead, he took up a new line of query.

"Had your Uncle any enemies that you know of?"

"I do not know exactly what you mean by enemies," replied Miss Pembroke; "owing to his unfortunate disposition, my uncle had no friends, but I do not know of anyone whom I would consider an aggressive enemy.

"Your uncle went to his room, you say, at about ten o'clock?"

"Yes, that was his usual hour for retiring."

"And after you yourself retired, did you hear anything in the night—any noise, that might have seemed unusual?"

"N—n—no," came a hesitating answer, after a considerable pause. Surely, no one could doubt that this girl was not telling all she knew! The evidence that she gave was fairly forced from her; it came hesitatingly, and her statements were unconvincing. She needed help, she needed counsel; she was too young and inexperienced to cope with the situation in which she found herself. But though I judged her thus leniently, the Coroner did not, and speaking almost sharply, he said:

"Consider carefully, Miss Pembroke. Are you sure you heard no noise in the night?"

Her calm seemed to have returned. "In an apartment house," she said, "there are always unexplainable noises. It is impossible to tell whether they come from the halls, the other apartments or the elevator. But I heard no noise that I considered suspicious or of evil import. Nothing to indicate what,—what must have taken place." She shuddered and buried her face in her hands as if to shut out an awful, imaginary sight.

"Then when you last saw or heard your uncle he was leaving you in a fit of rage?"

"Yes."

When Janet said this her eyes filled with tears, and I could readily understand how it hurt the tender-hearted young girl to remember that her uncle's last words to her had been uttered in anger. This, however, did not seem to affect the coroner. He went steadily on, with his voice singularly lacking in inflections.

"What did you do after your uncle retired?"

"I sat in the drawing-room and read for an hour or so."

"And then?"

"Then I put out the lights and went to bed."

Janet seemed to think that this ended her examination, and started to return to her seat; but the coroner stopped her.

"Miss Pembroke," he said, "I must ask you a few more questions. Where was your servant?"

"She had gone to bed some time earlier—about nine o'clock, I should say."

"So that after your uncle left you you were alone?"

"Yes."

"And when you went to bed you put out the lights for the night?"

"Yes."

"You——" The coroner hesitated for the fraction of a second, and then cleared his throat and went on: "You put the night-chain on the front door?"

"Yes." Janet spoke as if the matter were of no importance.

"Then—pardon me, Miss Pembroke—but if you put the chain on last night, at eleven, and Charlotte took it off this morning, at eight, how was it possible for a marauder to enter, as the inspector tells me he finds all the windows fastened, except those which Charlotte says she opened herself this morning?"

"I don't know," said Janet, the dazed look returning to her pale face, and then, sinking to the floor, she again swooned away.

IX

GEORGE LAWRENCE

The implication was awful, monstrous, and yet—there it was. Since, as Janet said, she put the chain on, and since it had been found still on by Charlotte in the morning, certainly no one could have entered the apartment during the night by that door. And as the apartment was the duplicate of our own, I knew there was no other door. There was no rear entrance, and the dumb-waiter closed with a snap lock on the kitchen side.

The inspector stated that the windows had evidently been securely fastened through the night. Those in the sleeping-rooms, which were partly opened for ventilation, were secured by a burglar-proof device, which fastened them at any desired point, leaving ample room for air, but far too small a space for a human being to pass through. Thus the possibility of an intruder was eliminated, and, granting that, who had killed Mr. Pembroke?

Logically speaking, it must have been some one already in the apartment, and the other occupants numbered but two. It didn't seem that it could have been Charlotte; and my mind refused even a hint of a thought of Janet in that connection; and yet—who?

As I sat stunned, I vaguely saw that some one had raised Miss Pembroke, and that Laura had once more taken her in charge.

I looked at the hard, impassive face of the coroner, and, like a flash, I realized that he believed Janet guilty, and that was why he had questioned her along the line he did.

He meant to prove first motive and then exclusive opportunity! I, as a lawyer, followed the workings of his mind, and understood at last his rigorous catechism of the poor girl.

Janet guilty! Why, it was simply a contradiction of terms. That girl was no more capable of—— Then I remembered her manner that had so puzzled me. But that she could explain, of course. As to exclusive opportunity, that was mere foolishness. I remembered the chained door, but of course there must have been other ways of ingress to a professional burglar. I hastily thought over the windows of our own apartment. There were three large front ones on Sixty-second Street, and the others were all on air-shafts or a fire-escape.

Ah, that was it—the fire-escape!

Then I remembered the inspector's statement. Had there been a possible way to get in that house that night, surely he would have found it. That would not require very clever detective work.

Suddenly a thought struck me, which turned my heart to ice. It was I who had first testified that the chain was on the door when Charlotte opened it that morning! If I had not mentioned it, perhaps no one would have thought of it, and it would have been assumed that the criminal forced his way in at the front door.

That would have left a loophole for doubt. Now they said there was none. Oh, how could I have been so stupid as to tell of that chain? I who desired only to serve and assist the woman I loved—I had done the one thing, said the one word, that gave those men reason to say she had "exclusive opportunity"!

That, then, was why Doctor Masterson had looked so perturbed at my testimony. That was why he was worried and nervous at Charlotte's mention of the chain. That was why he looked relieved when Laura completed her account without referring to that awful bit of evidence.

And why didn't Laura refer to it? Perhaps she thought it would be a point which couldn't be explained, which was as inexplicable to her as to me, but which no more proved Miss Pembroke guilty than it proved the angels in heaven to be criminals.

Janet had regained consciousness, but still lay on the couch, with closed eyes, and the inexorable coroner called George Lawrence.

The young man seemed to be controlling himself by a mighty effort.

"I see your implication," he said to the coroner, "and I want you to retract it. My cousin, Miss Pembroke, is incapable of such a thing as you hint, and the mere fact of a chained front door does not preclude other modes of housebreaking. I am by no means sure the windows were all securely fastened last night. Indeed, I am forced to believe they were not, since somebody came in and killed my uncle, and it was not my cousin Janet."

"There has been no accusation," said the coroner coldly. "Will you now give us your testimony?"

"I can tell you nothing to throw any light on the mystery," said George Lawrence, who was, apparently, holding himself well in hand. "I called here yesterday afternoon between five and six. My uncle was very cross and grumpy, and gave me no pleasant word while I was here. He was not at that time definitely angry, but merely testy and irritable. I talked for a time with Janet, and went away about six.

"Where did you go then?"

"I went back to my own apartment in Washington Square."

"And then?"

53

"I dressed, and went to dine with some friends in Sixtieth street. Of course this can be verified."

Lawrence spoke with an air of superciliousness, almost contempt, at this detailed questioning, but the Coroner looked at him impassively.

"We are not doubting your word," he said; "you spent the evening at the house where you dined?"

"Yes; I left there at eleven o'clock, and then I went directly home. I reached my apartment at eleven twenty-five."

"How do you know the time so exactly?"

"I happen to be sure of the hour, because the hall boy told me the time by the office clock. He then took me up in the elevator, and I went at once to my rooms. I slept all night, and had not yet left my bedroom when my cousin telephoned for me this morning. That is my story, and, as I said, it throws no light on the case. But light shall be thrown on the case, if I have to move heaven and earth to have it thrown. This mystery shall be solved and my cousin freed from the slightest taint of this absurd suspicion!"

I had liked George Lawrence from the first, and this outburst of loyalty to his cousin quite won my heart. It was no more than he ought to have felt, but his spontaneous enthusiasm charmed me. I determined to add my efforts to his own, and it would go hard if between us we did not bring the evil-doer to justice.

I admired the appearance of the young man. Of an athletic type, though perhaps not specially trained, he was well set up, and had that assured air that belongs to so many young New York men.

He especially exhibited self-possession and self-control, and though perhaps he gave more the effect of physical force than of mental strength, yet to my mind he showed bravery and courage both in manner and speech.

Though in no way conspicuous, his clothes were correct, and hung well on his rather graceful figure. Although I had heard he was an artist, he showed no trace of Bohemianism in his make-up. He was rather, it seemed to me, of the type that frequents our best clubs or restaurants.

But what I liked best about the man was his very evident affection and loyalty toward his cousin. As the coroner had said, there had been no definite accusation, and yet it was plain to be seen that as the evidence seemed to point toward either the guilt or the complicity of Janet Pembroke, the jurymen were being influenced by it.

The coroner asked George more questions.

"You carry a latch-key to this apartment?" he asked.

"Yes. I lived here until a few months ago, and I've still kept the key. I go in and out as I like. The chain is never put on in the daytime."

"Is it always on at night?"

"Yes. When I lived here I was usually the last one in at night, and I put on the chain. Since I left, my cousin has told me that she always puts it on when she retires at night."

"You did not get on well with your uncle?"

"I did not. It was because of his bad temper that I went away to live by myself. I hoped, too, that if I were not here to anger him, which I often did, he might be more gentle to Janet."

"Did it turn out that way?"

"I fear not, to any considerable extent. I think he could not control his temper, even if he tried, and it was his custom to vent his wrath on whomever happened to be nearest."

"You also knew of the conditions of your uncle's will?"

"Yes. It was no secret. He had always told us we two were his sole heirs, but, though he seemed willing to leave us his money, he was not generous with it while alive."

"What is your business, Mr. Lawrence?"

"I am an artist—or, at least, an illustrator. I make pictures for books and magazines."

"You find it lucrative?"

"Sufficiently so. My tastes are not extravagant, and I earn enough by my work to gratify my simple ambitions. I trust I shall make a worthy use of my inheritance, but I had hoped not to come into it for many years yet."

This last remark jarred on me. I didn't want to think the young man hypocritical, and yet that attitude as to his inheritance seemed to me not quite ingenuous.

"Did Robert Pembroke have any enemy that you know of?"

"Not that I know of definitely, and none that I would suspect of crime. But I know very little of my uncle's business affairs or his acquaintances. He was not at all communicative, and I was not curious about such matters."

"He had callers occasionally?"

"Yes."

"Of what sort?"

"Business men, his lawyer, various agents who transacted business for him, and sometimes strangers who came to ask contributions for charitable purposes, or perhaps to interest him in financial schemes."

"He always saw these visitors?"

"Yes; Mr. Pembroke was always ready to see any one who

called. I suppose, as he never went out, it provided diversion and entertainment for him."

"He always treated them politely?"

"Perhaps not that, but he was decent to them. However, he frequently used them as targets for his ill temper."

"They resented this?"

"That depended on their errand. If they were asking favors, they were naturally more patient than if they were there to transact my uncle's business."

"Your uncle also vented his ill-temper on his servants, I understand?"

"He certainly did. No servant ever staid very long in his employ."

"Can you think of any servant who has lived with him who might be implicated in this crime?"

George Lawrence paused, and seemed to be thinking over the line of servants who had come and gone. At last he shook his head; "Not definitely," he said. "I don't remember them individually. But there were several who were so badly treated by my uncle that it would not be surprising if they had held revengeful thoughts toward him. However, I could not go so far as to accuse any one of them."

"And you can't throw any light on these various articles collected from Mr. Pembroke's bedroom, and which we hope will prove to be clues to the discovery of the criminal."

Although the Coroner's words were straightforward enough, the glance he cast on the various articles I had laid before him, proved that he had little serious hope of assistance from them.

George Lawrence was even more plainly of an opinion that they were valueless. He glanced at them with an air of utter indifference, saying: "I really know nothing of them, I assure you."

"You have no idea who is the J. S. who signed his initials to this telegram?"

To my surprise, and I doubt not, also to the surprise of all present, George Lawrence turned to his cousin and smiled. It was a flashing smile, as if caused by a humorous thought, and it seemed so out of key with the proceedings, that it jarred on my sense of the fitness of things.

But I was even more surprised when Miss Pembroke flashed back an answering smile, showing entire comprehension of her cousin's meaning.

"You know something of the matter," affirmed the coroner, looking a little annoyed at the attitude of his witness.

"I am not sure that I do," said Lawrence, "but I will tell you what is in my mind. For many years my uncle lived in fear of a

56

personage whom he called J. S. Though rarely in humorous mood, my uncle would sometimes make jesting references to this J. S., as if he were in fear of him. When we asked him what name the initials stood for, he told us John Strong, but told us in such a way that he gave us clearly to understand that was not the real name of J. S. And so we came to look upon John Strong as a sort of mythical personage, and as the only one of whom my uncle was afraid. He has sometimes said to us, 'J. S. will catch me yet, if I'm not careful,' or, 'J. S. must never know of this.' It is our opinion, though uncorroborated by any known facts, that this man was once a partner of my uncle in business."

"A long time ago?"

"Yes; many years ago. These matters should be explained to you by my uncle's lawyer, but since he is not here, I will tell you what I know of this thing, though it is not much. As nearly as I could piece it together from the few hints my uncle let fall, I gathered that he and this J. S. bought a cotton plantation together, many years ago. At first the investment was unsuccessful. Then my uncle bought out John Strong's share, and after that the property became exceedingly valuable. I am perfectly sure my uncle dealt justly by his partner so far as the legality of the transaction was concerned. But John Strong seemed to think that my uncle was under a sort of moral obligation to give him a portion of the later profits. Now this is all I know about it, and I am not sure that these details are quite accurate. But I do know that the partner's name was not really John Strong, and that my uncle used that name because the man had a strong hold over him in some way."

"But you think the partner's initials were J. S.?"

"I think so, yes; but I am not sure."

"You have never seen the man?"

"Not to my knowledge. My uncle often had callers who were strangers to my cousin and myself."

"This matter seems to me to be important," said the Coroner, looking again at the telegram which was signed J. S.; "This message is dated yesterday and advised Mr. Pembroke to 'expect J. S. tonight,' that is, last evening. It certainly must be looked into."

"It certainly should," agreed George Lawrence. "When you have as evidence a telegram from a man known to be an enemy, it seems as if it ought to be investigated."

"But, on the other hand," went on the Coroner, looking very serious, "we know that this J. S. did not come last evening, in accordance with his announcement. We have Miss Pembroke's evidence, in addition to that of the servant, that there was no caller here last evening. Then after Miss Pembroke put the night-chain on the door and retired, there was no possibility of the entrance of an intruder. Therefore, we are bound to conclude that J. S. did not keep his engagement with Mr. Pembroke,—if indeed this is a genuine message from him."

At this remark of the Coroner's I looked aghast. He had practically cast a doubt on the genuineness of the telegram, and this implied that it was manufactured evidence, and so pointed to deeper and more complicated villainy than the crime itself. Moreover Mr. Ross's face expressed incredulity at the whole story of the mythical John Strong.

I was indignant at this, for the very frankness with which Lawrence told the story, the unmistakable approval and agreement of Janet in all that he said, and the slightly amused air of both of them all seemed to me to prove that the John Strong episode, whether important or not, whether for or against the cause I had espoused, was at least a true story, and honestly set forth.

But there was no doubt that the Coroner, the Inspector, and the Jurymen, took views entirely opposite to my own.

"I have heard your story, Mr. Lawrence," Mr. Ross said, calmly, "and the jurors have heard it It is recommended to their thoughtful consideration. The telegram signed J. S., may or may not be from this person whom you call John Strong, but whose name you say is something different. However as this person did not call last evening before Miss Pembroke put the chain on the front door, and as he could not have entered this apartment afterward, I cannot feel that we should attach great importance to this message. The evidence given goes to prove that the crime must have been committed after eleven o'clock last night, and, in the opinion of the doctors, by or before midnight. This narrows the time down to a very definite hour, and we see that the deed must have taken place shortly after Miss Pembroke had retired for the night."

George Lawrence was then excused from the witness stand, the inquest was closed, and the jurors dismissed to consider their verdict.

X

PERSON OR PERSONS UNKNOWN

I am usually cool-headed and clear-sighted, but as I realized the significance of the trend of the coroner's investigation my brain began to whirl. While I couldn't for a moment imagine Janet guilty of crime, or assistance or connivance thereat, there was much about the girl that I could not understand. Her sudden fainting spells and her spasms of convulsive weeping contrasted strangely with her calm, cold demeanor as she talked about her uncle. She had shown no grief at his death, but, remembering his cruelty to her I could not wonder at this. Surely, if ever a woman had cause to be glad at a relative's death, she had; and yet—what was I thinking of? Of course Janet, as I had already begun to hope I might some day call her— was incapable of anything but the gentlest and most filial thoughts of her dead uncle. Then my legal mind awoke again, and I said to myself: "I know absolutely nothing of this girl, or of her real nature. I am in love with her, I admit, but I have never spoken with her before today; she is a veritable stranger to me, and I cannot know the secrets of her heart."

Then the thought again occurred to me that, whatever might be the truth of the matter, I had been the one who first called attention to the chain on the door, which was, of course, the unassailable point against Janet. Since, therefore, I was directly responsible for this bit of evidence, which might or might not have been brought out otherwise, I felt that I owed all assistance in my power to the girl I had so unwittingly placed in an awkward predicament.

Foreseeing what the verdict of the coroner's jury must inevitably be, I formed my resolve at once. I sat down beside Janet and talked to her in a low tone.

"Miss Pembroke," I said, "the unfortunate circumstances of the case will undoubtedly lead to a trial before a legal jury. This may— though I trust it won't—cause you some annoyance, and in a merely nominal and formal way you may be held in detention for a few days. I wish, therefore, to ask if you have a family lawyer to whom you would naturally intrust the whole matter?"

"No," said Janet, and again I was repelled by her cold and unresponsive manner; "I know of no lawyer whom I would wish to consult; nor do I see any necessity for such consultation."

"Would you not wish to employ Mr. Leroy in this matter?"

I made this remark entirely from a sense of duty, for it seemed to me that the lawyer of the late Mr. Pembroke was the proper one to look after the affairs of his niece. And I had a secret sense of virtue rewarded, when I saw on Janet's face a look of utter repugnance to my suggestion.

"Indeed, no," she said, "in no circumstances could I think of consulting Mr. Leroy, or allowing him to advise me."

"Why not?" I asked, so impulsively, that I did not realize how blunt my words sounded. Indeed, I was so delighted at Janet's positive repudiation of the idea that I scarce knew what I was saying.

"Pardon me if I refuse to discuss my reasons with a stranger," was the answer, given in a haughty tone and with a distinct implication that I had overstepped the bounds of convention.

"You need not tell me why," I said earnestly, "but, Miss Pembroke, let me impress upon you the advisability of your seeing some one who has legal knowledge, and who can be of assistance to you in your present position."

Janet Pembroke looked at me with an expression on her face which I could not understand. We were sitting a little apart from the rest; Laura had risen and crossed the room to talk with George Lawrence, and as Miss Pembroke and I conversed in low tones, we were overheard by no one.

"I have my cousin to help me," she said, after a moment's pause; "and I will help him. We are both saddened by Uncle Robert's death, for though unkind to us, he was our relative, and as a family, we Pembrokes are of loyal instinct. And so Mr. Lawrence and myself are sufficient to each other, I think. There will be no question of financial settlements, as I know my uncle's will is definite. And as it is in the possession of Mr. Leroy, of course he will look after that matter. But George will be executor of the estate, that I know, and he and Mr. Leroy will attend entirely to carrying out my uncle's will, without necessity of my personal attention to the matter."

I was at a loss to know just how to intimate to the girl the serious position in which I felt sure she was about to be placed. Apparently she had not a clear appreciation of the Coroner's suspicions, which were only too evident to me. I was not sure that I ought to enlighten her, and yet it seemed to me that it would be better for her to be warned. I know that she would have to have a lawyer's assistance, whether she wanted it or not; and moreover, I wanted to be that lawyer. And, aside from this, I had the ever recurring remembrance that I was personally responsible for the evidence of the night-chain, and that it was that particular bit of evidence that had turned suspicion toward Janet.

But before offering my own services, I determined to make one more effort to persuade her to retain Leroy, for I knew that such a course would seem to anyone else the most rational and natural.

"At risk of offending you," I said; "I must urge you, Miss Pembroke, to follow my advice in regard to a lawyer. Will you not, at least, discuss the matter with Mr. Leroy as soon as he returns to the city?"

As I had feared, this made Miss Pembroke exceedingly angry. She did not raise her voice, in fact, she spoke in even a lower tone, but with a tense inflection that proved the depth of her feeling. Also, her face turned white, her red lips pressed closely together, and her dark eyes flashed as she replied: "Will you never understand, Mr. Landon, that I absolutely refuse to have any dealings with Graham Leroy? Entirely aside from my personal attitude toward the man, I know him to be unworthy of confidence or trust."

"Graham Leroy untrustworthy!" I exclaimed; "I am sure, Miss Pembroke, your personal prejudice makes you unjust to a well-known and even celebrated lawyer."

I regretted the words the moment I had spoken them. They were forced from me by an impulse of justice and generosity toward my rival, but even as I uttered them, I feared the effect they would have on the turbulent mind of the beautiful girl who was facing me.

And then again I was treated to one of the surprises that were ever in store for him who undertook to understand Janet Pembroke. Instead of resenting my speech, and flinging back some angry or haughty reply, she said, very gently:

"Ah, I see you do not know him,—at least, not as I do. I have known Mr. Leroy so long, and so well, that I know much about him that other people do not know. He was exceedingly intimate with my Uncle Robert. He is a man of brilliant mind, of remarkable talent; but he is crafty and even unscrupulous in his legal manœuvers. It may be that this was partly because of his deference to my uncle's wishes. Though Uncle Robert was himself honorable, so far as exact legality was concerned, yet I have cause to know that he allowed Mr. Leroy to carry on transactions for him that were,—— but why should I say this to you? I did not mean to! you have fairly dragged it out of me!"

Again her eyes were blazing with anger, and by a curious association of ideas, I suddenly remember, that I had once said to sister Laura that I would like to see this girl in a towering rage. Well, I was justified in my supposition! Her strange, almost weird beauty was enhanced by her intense emotion.

I spoke to her quietly. "You have done no harm in speaking to me thus; Graham Leroy is an acquaintance of mine, and a brother lawyer, but I have no personal friendship with him. I only suggested your consulting him, because it seemed to me right that you should do so."

"I thank you, Mr. Landon, for the interest you have shown in my affairs, and I am sure you will excuse me if I beg of you not to trouble yourself further about me."

Her sudden change of manner, from a gentle confidence to extreme hauteur warned me that she was about to conclude the interview, and that if I wished to carry my point, I must make a bold plunge. So, with an intonation scarcely less frigid than her own, I said:

"But—excuse me, Miss Pembroke, I feel it my duty to tell you that in all probability there will be a necessity for you to have the counsel of an experienced lawyer; and, since you have no one else at hand, I want to offer you my services. Do not think me presumptuous, but believe that I will do my best to serve you, and—that you will need such service."

The girl looked at me as if unable to comprehend my full meaning.

"Do I understand," she said slowly, "that because the apartment was locked and chained so that no one could enter, it may be supposed that I killed Uncle Robert?"

"You must admit," I replied, "that to a jury of disinterested outsiders it might seem to be a possibility."

"I!" she said, with a proud gesture and a look of hauteur even more scornful than she had previously shown; then with a sudden and complete change of demeanor she cried out brokenly: "Ah, well, perhaps I did!" and buried her face in her hands.

I was dumfounded. Her rapid alternations between an aggressive self-assurance and a nervous collapse left me more than ever uncertain as to the true nature of the woman.

But so deeply was I interested that this very uncertainty only whetted my desire to take up the case that I felt sure was more than probably impending.

"Never mind about that," I said calmly, "but please agree, Miss Pembroke, to consider me as your counsel from this moment."

This was, of course, precipitate, but I was impelled to it by the emergency of the moment. And, too, the conviction was every moment sinking deeper in my heart that this was the one woman in the world I could ever love. So alone was she, and so pathetic in her loneliness, so mysterious was her conduct and so fascinating her personality, that I resolved to devote all the legal talent I possessed to her aid.

"I will," she said, and she gave me a glance earnest but so inscrutable that I could make no guess as to its meaning.

If I was surprised at her quick acceptance of my offer, I made no sign of it. I had gained my point, and, satisfied, I said no more. Nor had I been mistaken in my premonitions.

The coroner's jury brought in a verdict that Robert Pembroke was murdered by some person or persons unknown, between the hours of eleven and one on Wednesday night. They suggested the detaining of Miss Pembroke and Charlotte, the maid, in custody of counsel who would be responsible for their appearance when called for.

As this was exactly the verdict I had expected, it was no surprise to me; but it acted like a thunder-bolt on the others.

George Lawrence was white with rage, and rather lost his head as he inveighed angrily against those who could be capable of such an absurdity as any connection between crime and Miss Janet Pembroke.

"Detain Janet!" he cried; "what nonsense!"

"It is not nonsense, Mr. Lawrence," said the coroner, "but we may call it merely a form, which is advisable in our opinion, until we can further investigate the case."

"Indeed we will investigate!" Lawrence declared; "and our investigation will prove that it was an intruder from outside who killed my uncle. A robber, a burglar, a professional criminal of some sort! You have enough evidence of this. Clues, you call them. Well, there they are; let them lead you to the discovery of the man who brought them here."

"But, Mr. Lawrence," objected the coroner, "it has been proved that a burglar, such as you speak of, could not get into this apartment last night. How do you suppose he entered?"

"How did he get in? I don't know! that is your business to find out. There you have your precious clues—enough of them to implicate any burglar. If necessary, get detectives—the best possible. Use any means, stop at no expense; but discover the man who committed this crime! And in the meantime, retract your absurd and idiotic suggestion of detaining Miss Pembroke."

Though not astonished that George Lawrence should so resent the suspicion of his cousin, I was surprised that he should express himself so vehemently and with such an exhibition of passion.

And then I remembered that both he and Miss Pembroke were of strongly emotional nature, and that since Robert Pembroke had been given to frequent exhibitions of anger and ill temper, it was probably an hereditary trait.

After the Coroner's words Lawrence said no more, but his

firmly set mouth and glaring eyes, betokened the intensity of his thoughts.

The colored girl, Charlotte, was also moved to loud and protesting lamentations. She became hysterical and wailed and moaned in true negro fashion.

"Oh, lawsy me!" she exclaimed! "why didn' I leave befoh dis yer strodegy happened! Oh, Miss Janet, honey, did yo' really kill Marse Robert? An' did you steal dat money? Oh, I nebber thought my Miss Janet would do dat!"

"Silence!" roared George Lawrence, but the excited woman paid no attention to him.

"She did, she did!" Charlotte went on; "Marse Robert, he told Miss Janet he'd cut her out of his will, ef she didn' marry that Leroy man! So, ob co'se, Miss Janet she jes' nachelly had to kill him!"

Although Charlotte's remarks were definite and dreadful, they were so incoherent and so interrupted by her wails and moans, that they made little impression on the people present. Moreover, George Lawrence had grasped the colored woman by the arm, and was shaking her into a submissive silence, threatening dire punishment, unless she ceased her random talk. I had gathered the trend of Charlotte's story; George and Janet had also understood it, but fortunately the Coroner and jurymen had been talking together, and had not listened to the servant's hysterical talk.

XI

THE CHAINED DOOR

Janet herself sat as one turned to stone. I think it was the first time she had realized that even a slight suspicion had definitely been attached to her name, and, had she been guilty, she could not have looked more stunned by shame and ignominy.

I remembered that she had said: "Perhaps I did do it"; I remembered that I knew nothing of her character save that it was a complex one, and—I wondered.

But it was no time for wondering; it was an occasion for action. Rising to my feet, I announced that as Miss Pembroke's counsel I would at once take up the direction of her affairs. I agreed to be responsible for her appearance, and Charlotte's also, whenever necessary, and I directed that any communication for Miss Pembroke be addressed to me as her lawyer.

My standing in my profession was of sufficient prominence to make all this possible, and the coroner agreed to my proposals.

George Lawrence looked amazed and not altogether pleased.

"I think, Janet," he said, "you should have left it to me to select your counsel."

As usual, Janet's behavior was an insoluble problem. "Why should I?" she retorted. "I need an able lawyer at once, and as Mr. Landon offered his services I was glad to accept his offer."

"What is your urgent need?" said George, looking at her peculiarly. "You are not accused."

"I may be," she returned calmly. "And, too, I have now important financial interests to be attended to."

I was shocked at the calm way in which she referred to her possible accusation, and also at the reference she made to her presumptive inheritance. Could it be, after all——?

"Yes," said George; "it is wise to have good legal advice immediately, and you have done well to retain Mr. Landon."

This sudden change of base surprised me, but I was growing used to surprises, and accepted it with the rest.

"Call on me," said George affably, as he held out his hand, "for any assistance or information I can give you regarding my cousin's affairs."

As it was then nearly two o'clock, I proposed to Laura that she take Miss Pembroke over to our own apartment for luncheon and rest, and, after a short talk with Mr. Lawrence, I would follow.

In conversation with George Lawrence, I learned that he was administrator of his uncle's estate, and as he and his cousin shared the inheritance equally, there would be little difficulty in the settling of financial affairs.

But as to the murder, there was more to be said.

George was still furious at the implication cast on Janet and continually repeated how absurd the whole idea was.

"But," I said, merely for argument's sake, "you know Miss Pembroke did put the chain on the door last night, and Charlotte did take it off this morning."

"There are other ways of getting in a house," stormed George. "Windows have been forced before now."

"Let us ourselves examine the windows," I said. "We may find some clue."

"I hate that word 'clue,'" he declared. "I hate all suggestion of detective work, and deductions, and inferences."

"But surely a detective is needed in a case like this," I said.

"Not to my notion. Uncle Robert was killed. Janet never killed him. Of course Charlotte didn't either. So somebody must have got in at the window."

"Very well then, a detective might find out who it was."

"Oh, detectives never find out anything. I did suggest employing them, I know; but I don't think they do any good. Now look at that bunch of stuff you picked up in my uncle's bedroom; surely that's enough for clues, if clues are wanted. But who could find the man who belongs to all that stuff?"

"I'm afraid, Mr. Lawrence you haven't a deductive mind. I'm no detective myself, but my legal training makes it natural for me to connect cause and effect. Apparently your mind doesn't work that way."

"No," said Lawrence, smiling; "I suppose I have what is called the artistic temperament. I am rather careless and inconsequent in my mental attitude, and I certainly never could reason out anything—let alone a gruesome mystery like this. But, for that matter, if you're going to look at the situation in the light of pure reason, it seems to me it's this way: The murderer of my uncle came in from the outside. He couldn't come through the door, therefore he came in through a window; and there you have the whole thing in a nutshell. Now, find your burglar."

I couldn't help feeling attracted to the young man. Although he spoke in a light tone, he was by no means unmindful of the gravity of the situation, and his only thought seemed to be to refute the absurd suspicion which had fallen on his cousin.

66

"But how could any one get in at a window?" I remonstrated. "The windows were all fastened."

"Don't ask me how he did it! I don't know. I only say he did do it, because he must have done it! If he left clues behind him, so much the better for the detectives. Those handkerchiefs and theater stubs mean nothing to me, but if they could put a detective on the right track I'll be only too glad to pay the gentleman's well-earned fee."

"What about the key?" I said. "Isn't that a clue?"

"Clue to what?" returned Lawrence; "it's probably my uncle's own key, that he had slipped under his pillow for safety."

"That's exactly what I think myself. How can we find out?"

"Well, I don't see how we can find out until Leroy comes home. I know the will makes me executor,—but of course, I can't do anything in that matter until my uncle's lawyer is present."

"Why not call up Leroy's office and find out when he's coming home?"

"Not a bad idea," agreed Lawrence, and putting the plan into action, we learned that Mr. Leroy was not expected back for two days at least. Whereupon we gave orders to his secretary to communicate with him at once, tell him of the tragedy, and urge his immediate return. This was promised, and then our conversation returned to the subject of the lawyer. I discovered at once that Lawrence did not like him, although his denunciation of Leroy was not so severe as Janet's. Indeed Lawrence's chief grievance against the lawyer seemed to be Leroy's desire to marry Janet.

"He's too old," he exclaimed, when I asked his reasons. "Just because he's a handsome, rich widower, all the women are crazy after him. But Janet isn't,—she detests him."

I knew this to be true from Miss Pembroke's own words, and at the risk of seeming intrusive, I pursued the subject further.

"Mr. Pembroke desired the match, didn't he?"

"Oh yes; Uncle Robert was hand and glove with Leroy. And what that fool colored woman said, was true; Uncle Robert had threatened to disinherit Janet if she persisted in refusing Leroy. But you know as well as I do, that that doesn't mean a thing in connection with the death of Uncle Robert."

"Of course not," I agreed, heartily. "By the way, of course no suspicion could be attached to Leroy?"

"Heavens, no! how utterly absurd! and yet——" Lawrence hesitated, and a strange look came into his eyes, "oh, pshaw! suspicion can be attached to anybody and to nobody! to anybody, that is, except Janet. To dream of her in such a connection is impossibility itself."

"Of course it is," I agreed; "and I don't think you need bother about those foolish remarks of Charlotte's, for I don't think Mr. Ross or his people heard them. By the way, when was Leroy here last?"

"Why, I don't know. Yes, I know he was here night before last because yesterday afternoon, Janet told me of the terrible scene they all had with uncle. He was in such a rage that Janet begged Mr. Leroy to go away."

"What an old Tartar that man was!" I exclaimed, my whole heart going out in sympathy to the poor girl who had borne such injustice and unkindness.

"He was all of that," assented Lawrence, "and in my secret heart I can't grieve very deeply because he's gone. But of course——"

"Of course his death must be avenged," I continued for him, "and proper measures must be taken, and at once."

"Yes, I suppose so," agreed Lawrence, with a sigh. "And I will do my part, whatever it may be. But I confess I have no taste for this investigation business. If you have, Landon, I wish to goodness you'd go ahead and examine the whole place to your heart's content. I'd be glad to have it done, but I can't bear to do it myself, and I'd take it kindly of you if you'd help me out."

At this, since George wouldn't accompany me, I myself thoroughly examined all the windows of the apartment. I have, I am sure, what is known as the "detective instinct." I am of the conviction that it is scarcely possible for a human being to be in a room, even for a short time, and go from it without leaving behind him some evidence of his having been there. So I made a round of the rooms. I scrutinized every window. The only ones I found open were those which Charlotte had said she had herself opened that morning. The others were securely fastened with an ingenious contrivance which was really burglar-proof. Granting Charlotte's assertions to be true, which I had no reason to doubt, the net was surely drawing closely around these two women. But I felt sure there was some other possibility, and I determined to discover it.

There was no back stair or kitchen exit. The dumb-waiter had a strong snap bolt and closed itself, without any means of opening from the other side. Then I returned and carefully examined the front door. The Hale lock, though easily opened with its own key, was not to be opened otherwise; and, aside from this, a key was of no use if the night-chain was on. I looked at the heavy brass chain; then I put it in its slot, and opened the door the slight distance that the chain allowed. The opening was barely large enough to admit my hand. There was no possibility of a man getting through that tiny crack, nor could he by any chance put his hand through and slide the chain back; for to remove the chain I had to close the door again, as Charlotte had done this morning.

For the first time I began to feel that I was really facing a terrible situation.

If only I had kept silent about that chain, and if Janet and Charlotte had also failed to mention it, there would have been ample grounds for suspecting that an intruder had come in by the front door.

But realizing myself that the windows had all been secured, and that the chain had been on all night, what possibility was left save the implication of one or both of the only human beings shut inside with the victim?

Bah! There must be other possibilities, no matter how improbable they might be. Perhaps an intruder had come in before the door was chained, and had concealed himself until midnight and then had committed the crime.

But I was forced to admit that he could not have put the chain on the door behind him when he went away.

I even tried this, and, of course, when the door was sufficiently ajar to get my hand through, I could not push the end of the chain back to its socket. The door had to be closed to do this.

With a growing terror at my heart, I reviewed other possibilities. Perhaps the intruder had remained in the house all night, and had slipped away unobserved in the morning.

But he couldn't have gone before Charlotte unchained the door, and since then there had been a crowd of people around constantly.

Still this must have been the way, because there was no other way. Possibly he could have remained in the house over night, and part of the morning, and slipped out during the slight commotion caused by the entrance of the jurymen. But this was palpably absurd, for with the jurors and the officials and the reporters all on watch, besides the doctors and ourselves, it was practically impossible that a stranger could make his escape.

Could he possibly be still concealed in the house? There were many heavy hangings and window curtains where such concealment would be possible, but far from probable. However, I made a thorough search of every curtained window and alcove, of every cupboard, of every available nook or cranny that might possibly conceal an intruder. The fact that the apartment was a duplicate of our own aided me in my search, and when I had finished, I was positive the murderer of Robert Pembroke was not hidden there.

My thoughts seemed baffled at every turn.

There was one other possibility, and, though I evaded it as long as I could, I was at last driven to the consideration of it.

The fact of the securely locked door and windows precluded any entrance of an intruder, unless he had been admitted by one of the three inhabitants of the apartment.

At first I imagined Robert Pembroke having risen and opened the door to some caller, but I immediately dismissed this idea as absurd. For, granting that he had done so, and that the caller had killed him, he could not have relocked the door afterward. This brought me to the thought I had been evading; could Charlotte or— or Janet have let in anybody who, with or without their knowledge, had killed the old man?

It seemed an untenable theory, and yet I infinitely preferred it to a thought of Janet's guilt.

And the worst part of this theory was that in some vague shadowy way it seemed to suggest Leroy.

Lawrence had acted peculiarly when I suggested Leroy's name in connection with our search. Janet had acted strangely whenever I mentioned Leroy; but for that matter, when did Janet not act strangely?

And though my thoughts took no definite shape, though I formed no suspicions and formulated no theories, yet I could not entirely quell a blurred mental picture of Janet opening the door to Leroy, and then—well,—and what then? my imagination flatly refused to go further, and I turned it in another direction.

I couldn't suspect Charlotte. Although she disliked her master, she hadn't sufficient strength of mind to plan or to carry out the deed as it must have been done.

No, it was the work of a bold, unscrupulous nature, and was conceived and executed by an unfaltering hand and an iron will.

And Janet? Had she not shown a side of her nature which betokened unmistakably a strength of will and a stolid sort of determination?

Might she not, in the wakeful hours of the night, have concluded that she could not stand her uncle's tyranny a day longer, and in a sudden frenzy been moved to end it all?

I pushed the thought from me, but it recurred again and again.

Her demeanor that morning, I was forced to admit, was what might have been expected, had she been guilty. Her swooning fits, alternating with those sudden effects of extreme haughtiness and bravado, were just what one might expect from a woman of her conflicting emotions.

That she had a temper similar in kind, if not in degree, to her late uncle's, I could not doubt; that she was impulsive, and could be irritated even to frenzy, I did not doubt; and yet I loved her, and I did not believe her guilty.

70

This was probably cause and effect, but never would I believe the girl responsible in any way for the crime until she told me so herself. But could she have been an accessory thereto, or could she have caused or connived at it? Could I imagine her so desperate at her hard lot as to—but pshaw! what was the use of imagining? If, as I had often thought, I had even a slight detective ability, why not search for other clues that must exist, and that would, at least, give me a hint as to which direction I might look for the criminal?

Determined, then, to find something further I went to Mr. Pembroke's bedroom. There I found Inspector Crawford on his hands and knees, still searching for the broken end of the hat-pin.

But, though we both went over every inch of the floor and furniture, nothing could be found that could be looked upon as a clue of any sort.

"Of course," I observed, "the intruder carried the end of the pin away with him, after he broke it off."

"What are you talking about?" almost snarled the inspector. "An intruder is a physical impossibility. Even the skeleton man from the museum couldn't slide through a door that could open only three inches. And, too, men don't wear hat-pins. It is a woman's weapon."

XII

JANET IS OUR GUEST

Ah, so the blow had fallen! He definitely suspected Janet, and, besides the point of evidence, opportunity, he condemned her in his own mind because a hat-pin pointed to a woman's work. He didn't tell me this in so many words—he didn't have to. I read from his face, and from his air of finality, that he was convinced of Janet's guilt, either with or without Charlotte's assistance.

And I must admit, that in all my thought and theory, in all my imagination and visioning, in all my conclusions and deductions, I had entirely lost sight of the weapon, and of the fact that the Inspector stated so tersely, that it was a woman's weapon. It was a woman's weapon, and it suddenly seemed to me that all my carefully built air-castles went crashing down beneath the blow!

"Well," I said, "Inspector, if you can't find the other half of the pin, it seems to me to prove that an intruder not only came in, but went away again, carrying that tell-tale pin-head with him,—or with her, if you prefer it. I suppose there are other women in the world, beside the lady you are so unjustly suspecting, and I suppose, too, if an intruder succeeded in getting in here, it might equally well have been a woman as a man."

Inspector Crawford growled an inaudible reply, but I gathered that he did not agree with me in any respect.

"And then again, Inspector," I went on, determined to talk to him while I had the chance, "if there was no intruder, where, in your opinion, do all those clues point to? Mr. Lawrence thinks them of little value, but as a detective, I'm sure you rate them more highly. Granting the hat-pin indicates a woman's work, what about the man's handkerchief?"

"No clues mean anything until they are run down," said Mr. Crawford, looking at me gravely; "I'm not sure that the handkerchief and ticket stubs and time-table, and all those things, weren't the property of Mr. Pembroke; but the only way to be sure is to trace them to their owner, and this is the next step that ought to be taken. This is not a simple case, Mr. Landon; it grows more complex every minute. And please remember I have not said I suspect Miss Pembroke, either of guilt or of complicity. She may be entirely innocent. But you must admit that there is sufficient circumstantial evidence to warrant our keeping her in view."

"There isn't any evidence at all, circumstantial or otherwise, against her!" I declared, hotly; "you merely mean that she was in this apartment and so had opportunity to kill her uncle if she wanted to. But, I repeat, you haven't a shred or a vestige of evidence,—real evidence,—against her."

"Well, we may have, after some further investigation. As you know, the whole matter rests now for a few days; at any rate, until after the funeral of Mr. Pembroke, and until after the return of Mr. Leroy."

"Do you know Graham Leroy?" I asked, suddenly.

It must have been my tone that betrayed my desire to turn suspicion in any new direction, for the Inspector's grey eyes gleamed at me shrewdly. "Don't let any foolishness of that kind run away with your wits," he said; "Graham Leroy is too prominent a man to go around killing people."

"That may be so; but prominence doesn't always preclude wrong doing," I said, rather sententiously.

"Well, don't waste time on Leroy. Follow up your clues and see where they lead you. Greater mysteries than this have been solved by means of even more trivial things than a handkerchief and a few bits of paper. To my mind, the absence of the other half of that hat-pin is the most remarkable clue we have yet stumbled upon. Why should the murderer break it off and carry it away with her?"

"The doctors have explained that because it was broken off, it almost disappeared from sight; and had it done so, the crime might never have been suspected. Surely this is reason enough for the criminal to take the broken pin away."

The Inspector nodded his head. "Sure," he agreed. "With the spectacular hat-pins the women wear nowadays it might have proved an easy thing to trace. However, it is necessary that I search all the rooms of this apartment for it."

This speech sent a shock through my whole being. I had searched the apartment, but it had been merely with the idea of noting the window fastenings, and looking for a possible villain hidden among the draperies. I had not thought of a search of personal belongings, or of prying into the boxes or bureau-drawers. And that odious Inspector doubtless meant that he would search Janet's room,—and for that hat-pin! Suppose he found it! But I would not allow myself such disloyalty even in imagination.

Changing the subject, I said, "do you think that key they found is Mr. Pembroke's?"

"I don't think anything about it, it isn't a matter of opinion. That key belonged either to the deceased or to somebody else. It's up to us to find out which, and not to wonder or think or imagine who it might, could, would or should have belonged to!"

Clearly, the Inspector was growing testy. I fancied he was not making as rapid progress as he had hoped, and I knew, too, he was greatly chagrined at not finding the pin. As he would probably immediately set about searching the whole place, and as I had no wish to accompany him on his prying into Janet's personal effects, I concluded to go home.

Sad at heart, I turned away from my unsuccessful search for clues, and, bidding good-by to George Lawrence and to the officials who were still in charge of the place, I crossed to my own apartment.

The contrast between the gruesome scenes I had just left and the cheery, pleasant picture that met my eyes as I entered thrilled me with a new and delightful sensation.

To see Janet Pembroke sitting in my own library, in one of my own easy chairs, gave me a cozy, homelike impression quite different from that of Laura's always busy presence around the house.

Miss Pembroke smiled as I entered, and held out her hand to me.

"Mrs. Mulford has been so good to me," she said. "She is treating me more like a sister than a guest, and I am not used to such kind care."

Although I was fascinated by Janet's smile and tone, I was again surprised at her sudden change of demeanor. She seemed bright and almost happy. What was the secret of a nature that could thus apparently throw off the effects of a recent dreadful experience and assume the air of a gentle society girl without a care in the world?

But I met her on her own grounds, and, shaking hands cordially, I expressed my pleasure at seeing her under my roof-tree.

She suddenly became more serious, and said thoughtfully:

"I don't see what I can do, or where I can live. I can't go back to those rooms across the hall"—she gave a slight shudder—"and I can't live with Cousin George now, and I can't live alone. Perhaps Milly Waring would take me in for a time."

"Miss Pembroke," I said, "I am, as you know, your counsel, and as such I must have a very serious talk with you."

"But not now," broke in Laura; "Miss Pembroke is not going to be bothered by any more serious talk until after she has eaten something. Luncheon is all ready, and we were only waiting for you to come, to have it served."

I was quite willing to defer the conversation, and, moreover, was quite ready myself for rest and refreshment.

Notwithstanding the surcharged atmosphere, the meal was a

pleasant one. Laura's unfailing tact prevented any awkwardness, and as we all three seemed determined not to refer to the events of the morning, the conversation was light and agreeable, though desultory.

"I wish I had asked Mr. Lawrence to come over to luncheon, too," said Laura. "Poor man, he must be nearly starved."

"Oh, George will look out for himself," said Janet. "But I hope he will come back here this afternoon, as I must talk to him about my future home."

"Miss Pembroke," I said, feeling that the subject could be evaded no longer, "I hope you can make yourself contented to stay here with my sister and myself for a time, at least. Of course it is merely nominal, but you must understand that you are detained, and that I, as your lawyer, am responsible for your appearance."

"Do you mean," asked Janet in her calm way, "that I'm under arrest?"

"Not that exactly," I explained. "Indeed, it is not in any sense arrest; you are merely held in detention, in my custody. I do not apprehend that your appearance in court will be necessary, but it is my duty to be able to produce you if called for."

Seeing that the serious consideration of Janet's affairs could be put off no longer, Laura proposed that we adjourn to the library and have our talk there.

"And I want to say, first of all," she began, "that I invite you, Miss Pembroke, to stay here for a time as my guest, without any question of nominal detention or any of that foolishness. Otis may be your counsel, and may look after your business affairs, but I am your hostess, and I'm going to take care of you and entertain you. If you are in any one's custody you are in mine, and I promise to 'produce you when you are called for.'"

If ever I saw gratitude on any human face, it appeared on Janet Pembroke's then. She grasped Laura by both hands, and the tears came to her eyes as she thanked my sister for her whole-souled kindness to an entire stranger.

"Surely," I thought to myself, "this is the real woman, after all; this grateful, sunny, warm-hearted nature is the real one. I do not understand the coldness and hardness that sometimes comes into her face, but I shall yet learn what it means. I have two problems before me; one to discover who killed Robert Pembroke, and the other to find the solution of that delightful mystery, Janet Pembroke herself."

I could see that Laura, too, had fallen completely under the spell of Janet's charm, and, though she also was mystified at the girl's sudden changes of manner, she thoroughly believed in her,

75

and offered her friendship without reserve. As for myself, I was becoming more infatuated every moment. Indeed, so sudden and complete had been my capitulation that had I been convinced beyond all doubt of Janet's guilt, I should still have loved her.

But as I was by no means convinced of it, my duty lay along the line of thorough investigation.

It having been settled, therefore, that Janet should remain with us for a time, I proceeded at once to ask her a few important questions, that I might at least outline my plan of defence, even before the real need of a defence had arisen.

"Of course you know, Miss Pembroke," said I, "that, as your lawyer, I shall do everything I can for you in this matter; but I want you to feel also that I take a personal interest in the case, and I hope you will trust me implicitly and give me your unlimited confidence."

"You mean," said Janet, who had again assumed her inscrutable expression, "that I must tell you the truth?"

I felt a little repulsed by her haughty way of speaking, and, too, I slightly dreaded the revelations she might be about to make; but I answered gravely: "Yes, as my client you must tell me the absolute truth. You must state the facts as you know them."

"Then I have simply nothing to tell you," said Janet and her face had the cold immobility of a marble statue.

"Perhaps I had better not stay with you during this conversation," said Laura, looking disturbed.

"Oh, do stay!" cried Janet, clasping her hands, as if in dismay. "I have nothing to say to Mr. Landon that you may not hear. Indeed, I have nothing to say at all."

"But you must confide in me, Miss Pembroke," I insisted. "I can do nothing for you if you do not."

"You can do nothing for me if I do," she said, and her words struck a chill to my heart. Laura, too, gave a little shiver and seemed instinctively to draw slightly away from Janet.

"I mean," Miss Pembroke went on hastily, "that I have nothing to tell you other than I have already told. I did put the chain on and put out the lights last night at eleven o'clock. I did fasten all of the windows—all of them. Charlotte did unfasten some of the windows between seven and eight this morning; she did unchain and open the door at about eight o'clock. Those are all the facts I know of. I did not kill Uncle Robert, and, of course, Charlotte did not."

"How do you know Charlotte did not?" I asked.

"Only because the idea is absurd. Charlotte has been with us but a short time, and expected to leave soon, any way. My uncle had been cross to her, but not sufficiently so to make her desire to kill him. He never treated her like he treated me!"

The tone, even more than the words, betrayed a deep resentment of her uncle's treatment of her, and as I found I must put my questions very definitely to get any information whatever, I made myself say: "Did you, then, ever desire to kill him?"

Janet Pembroke looked straight at me, and as she spoke a growing look of horror came into her eyes.

"I have promised to be truthful," she said, "so I must tell you that there have been moments when I have felt the impulse to kill Uncle Robert; but it was merely a passing impulse, the result of my own almost uncontrollable temper. The thought always passed as quickly as it came, but since you ask, I must admit that several times it did come."

Laura threw her arms around Janet with a hearty caress, which I knew was meant as an atonement for the shadow of doubt she had recently felt.

"I knew it!" she exclaimed. "And it is your supersensitive honesty that makes you confess to that momentary impulse! Any one so instinctively truthful is incapable of more than a fleeting thought of such a wrong."

I think that at that moment I would have given half my fortune to feel as Laura did; but what Janet had said did not seem to me so utterly conclusive of her innocence. Indeed, I could not evade an impression that sudden and violent anger was often responsible for crime, and in case of a fit of anger intense enough to amount practically to insanity, might it not mean the involuntary and perhaps unremembered commission of a fatal deed? This, however, I immediately felt to be absurd. For, though a crime might be committed on the impulse of a sudden insanity of anger, it could not be done unconsciously. Therefore, if Janet Pembroke was guilty of her uncle's death, directly or indirectly, she was telling a deliberate falsehood; and if she was not guilty, then the case was a mystery that seemed insoluble. But insoluble it should not remain. I was determined to pluck the heart out of this mystery if it were in power of mortal man to do so. I would spare no effort, no trouble, no expense. And yet, like a flash, I foresaw that one of two things must inevitably happen: should I be able to prove Janet innocent, she should be triumphantly acquitted before the world; but if, on the contrary, there was proof to convince even me of her guilt, she must still be acquitted before the world! I was not so inexperienced in my profession as not to know just what this meant to myself and to my career, but I accepted the situation, and was willing, if need be, to take the consequences.

These thoughts had crowded upon me so thick and fast that I was unconscious of the long pause in the conversation, until I was recalled to myself by an instinctive knowledge that Janet was gazing at me. Meeting her eyes suddenly, I encountered a look that seemed to imply the very depths of sorrow, despair, and remorse.

"You don't believe in me," she said, "and your sister does. Why do you doubt my word?"

I had rapidly come to the conclusion that the only possible attitude to adopt toward the strange nature with which I had to deal was that of direct plainness.

"My sister, being a woman, is naturally guided and influenced by her intuitions," I said; "I, not only as a man but as a lawyer, undertaking a serious case, am obliged to depend upon the facts which I observe for myself, and the facts which I gather from the statements of my client."

"But you don't believe the facts I state," said Janet and now her tone acquired a petulance, as of a pouting child.

I was annoyed at this, and began to think that I had to deal with a dozen different natures in one, and could never know which would appear uppermost. I returned to my inquisition.

"Why do you think Charlotte could not have done this thing?" I asked, although I had asked this before.

"Because she had no motive," said Janet briefly.

This was surprising in its implication, but I went doggedly on:

"Who, then, had a motive?"

"I can think of no one except George Lawrence and myself." The troubled air with which Janet said this seemed in no way to implicate either her cousin or herself, but rather suggested to me that she had been pondering the subject, and striving to think of some one else who might have had a motive.

"And you didn't do it," I said, partly by way of amends for my own doubtful attitude, "and George Lawrence couldn't get in the apartment, unless——"

"Unless what?" asked Janet, looking steadily at me.

"Unless you or Charlotte let him in."

I was uncertain how Janet would take this speech. I even feared she might fly into a rage at my suggestion, but, to my surprise, she answered me very quietly, and with a look of perplexity: "No, I didn't do that, and I'm sure Charlotte didn't either. She had no motive."

Again that insistence on motive.

"Then the facts," I said bluntly, "narrow themselves down to these. You say that you know of only yourself and Mr. Lawrence to whom motive might be attributed. Evidence shows only yourself and Charlotte to have had opportunity. Believing, as I thoroughly do, that no one of the three committed the murder, it shall be my task to discover some other individual to whom a motive can be ascribed, and who can be proved to have had opportunity."

At this speech Janet's face lighted up with a brightness that was like a glory. A look of relief, hope, and gladness came into her eyes, and so beautiful did she appear that again I said to myself that this was indeed her real nature; that she had been nearly tortured to death by her dreadful uncle, and that when the mystery was solved and the dreadful tragedy a thing of the past this was the way she would appear always. More than ever I determined to find out the truth, and bring to justice the evil-doer. Alas! how little I thought what would be the sad result of my search for truth!

XIII

JANET IS MYSTERIOUS

"How clearly you put it!" exclaimed Janet in response to my last statement. "That is exactly what we have to do. Find some other person who had a motive, and who must have found an opportunity."

"I will," I vowed, earnestly, "but it will help me so much if you can only bring yourself to trust me more fully. You know, you must know, that I have only your good at heart."

I should have stopped right here, but it chanced that just at that moment Laura was called away on some household affair and left me alone with Janet. So, acting on an uncontrollable impulse, I said further: "I think if you knew how fervently I desire to do all I can for you, you would look upon me more in the light of a friend."

"Are you my friend?" and Janet Pembroke's dark eyes looked into mine with a wistful gaze and an expression of more gentleness than I had thought the girl capable of. And yet I felt an intuitive certainty that if I met that expression with a similar one, she would at once flash back to her haughty demeanor and inscrutable air.

"I am your friend," I said, but said it with a frank straightforwardness, which I hoped would appeal to her.

But, alas, I had chosen the wrong manner; or I had made a mistake somewhere, for the wistfulness died out of her eyes and her lip curled disdainfully.

"You're not a friend," she stated, calmly; "you are my lawyer, I have employed you as such; and when your work is finished, I shall pay you your fees. I trust you will use your best efforts in my behalf, and I may say I have confidence in your knowledge and your skill in your profession."

I have heard of people who felt as if they had been douched with cold water, but I felt as if I had been overwhelmed by an icy avalanche! I had no idea why the sudden change occurred in her treatment of me, but I was determined to meet her on her own ground. Moreover, my interest was rather piqued at her strange behavior, and I was not at all sorry that I was to carry on the case for this wilful beauty.

"I thank you, Miss Pembroke," I said in my most coldly polite manner, "for the confidence you express in my ability to handle your case; and I assure you I shall put forth my best efforts in anything I can or may do for you. As I told you, it would help us both if you were more frank with me,—but that is as you choose."

"It isn't as I choose!" the girl burst forth, "I am forced,—forced by circumstances to act as I do! I would willingly tell you all, but I cannot,—I cannot! Mr. Landon, you must believe me!"

"I do believe you," I exclaimed, softened at once by her pained outcry. "I confess I cannot understand you, but I will promise to believe you."

"I cannot understand myself," she said, slowly, and again a trace of that wistfulness showed in her eyes and in her drooping mouth. "I do so want a friend."

Was the girl a coquette? was she leading me on, purposely, and enjoying my bewilderment at her sudden transitions of mood?

At any rate she should not fool me twice in the same way. Not again would I offer her my friendship to have it scornfully rejected.

"I think you do need a friend, Miss Pembroke," I said in a tone, which I purposely made very kind; "and I can assure you you will find a true one in my sister, Mrs. Mulford. I know she is already fond of you, and it rests with yourself whether or not she is your firm and faithful friend."

As I said this, I rose, for I was just about to go away to my office, where some urgent business required my immediate attention. I had intended a very formal leave-taking, but to my surprise, Janet rose too, and putting out both hands said, "Thank you, Mr. Landon,—very deeply. I shall be only too glad to be friends with your sister, if she will give her friendship to a girl so unfortunately placed as myself."

This remark could have called forth various kinds of response. But I knew it wiser to indulge in none of them, and with a formal, "good afternoon," I went away.

There was business that required my presence at my office that afternoon, but I went also to get an opportunity to think by myself about the case I had undertaken. I seemed to have entered upon a new phase of existence, and one which was maddeningly contradictory. Above all else, I was surprised by the fact that I had fallen so suddenly and irrevocably in love. As I had reached the age of thirty-two without a serious love affair, I had come to the conclusion that my fate was to lead a bachelor life. But with Laura to look after me I had not felt this a deprivation. Now, however, all was changed, and I knew that unless I first cleared Janet's name from all taint of suspicion, and then won her for my wife, I should never know another happy hour.

Although I intended to think over the legal aspects and the significant facts of the case I had undertaken, I found myself instead

81

indulging in rose-colored dreams of what might happen in the future. It was perhaps the buoyant hopefulness consequent upon my realization of my love for Janet, but at any rate I felt not the slightest doubt that I should be able to free her entirely from any hint of suspicion.

The fact that she was a mystery, that I could not understand her behavior or sound the depths of her nature, in no way detracted from my admiration of her. Indeed it rather whetted my interest and made all other women seem ordinary and tame by comparison. I deliberately assured myself that I had gone thus far through the world, heart free, for the very reason that never before had I met a woman who was out of the ordinary. Then, too, Janet's beauty was of no usual type. Other women might possess dark eyes and hair, red lips and a perfect complexion, but surely no one else ever had so expressive a face, where the emotions played in turn, each more beautiful than the last.

Had I seen only her exhibitions of pride, anger or dismay, I might not have been so attracted; but having caught that fleeting smile of wistfulness, and that wonderful gaze of gentleness, I was fully determined to win her for my own, and to make those expressions the usual ones on her beloved face.

The question of her possible guilt or complicity in guilt bothered me not at all. I knew she was innocent, and my only problem now was how to prove it to an unjust and suspicious world. But it should be done, for I would devote my best and bravest efforts to the cause, and I felt sure of ultimate triumph.

If the thought obtruded itself on my mind that circumstances were against me, that my way would be a difficult one, and that even I myself were I not blinded by love, must feel some doubts, I resolutely ignored it, and resolved to succeed in spite of it.

But I knew that the work I had undertaken would require not only the exercise of my highest legal powers, but also my most dextrous and ingenious methods of handling.

I therefore looked after only such other matters as required my immediate attention, and then gave myself up unreservedly to the Pembroke case. Although technically it could not yet be called a case, I well knew if no other important evidence was brought out Janet would certainly be arrested, at least for complicity. Others might not believe her statement that she did not open the door to any one that night. As for myself, I did not know whether I believed it or not, and, furthermore, I did not care. I had determined to accept all Janet said as true, for a working basis. Let the results be what they might, let the truth be what it would, I would clear her name before the world, in defiance, if necessary, of my own beliefs.

I set myself to work, and, with all the ingenuity acquired by my legal training, endeavored to construct a case. But it was by far the most difficult task I had ever attempted. The facts were so few and so evidential that it seemed to be an occasion for two and two making four, and possessing no ability to make anything else. Clearly I must collect more evidence, if—and though I didn't say this even to myself, I admit it haunted my brain—even if it had to be manufactured!

But this was absurd; there was no occasion to manufacture evidence, all I had to do was to go and get it. There were the several clues that I had myself discovered, yet to be traced to their source.

And yet, though I couldn't myself understand why, those clues seemed to promise little. I thought of those engaging detectives in fiction, how with one or two tiny clues they are enabled to walk straight to the murderer's front door and ring his bell. Yet here was I, with half a dozen clues at my disposal, and they seemed to me not at all indicative of the murderer's whereabouts.

I wouldn't admit it to myself, but of course the truth must be, that since Mr. Pembroke had been murdered while the only entrance to the house was securely fastened, those precious clues could not have been left there by the criminal! If this disheartening thought attempted to present itself, I promptly thrust it aside, and remembered only that I had the clues, if they were clues, and certainly they did not point toward Janet.

What had been called the principal clue, the hat-pin, the woman's weapon,—I ignored. I was not considering anything that pointed in a direction I did not choose to look.

That was probably the real reason why I did not go at once for a professional detective and give him free rein. I knew he would begin on the hat-pin, and would end—, well,—never mind that.

As a beginning, I made a list of matters to be investigated, setting them down, in my methodical way, in the order of their discovery.

I had the key, the theatre stubs, the time-table, the torn telegram and the handkerchief. Surely, a lengthy list. Of course there had also been a hair-pin,—an ordinary wire hair-pin,—but this, I omitted for reasons of my own.

Aside from the fact that it headed the list, the key seemed to me the most important. It was doubtless the key to some one of Mr. Pembroke's deposit boxes. And if so, it should prove useful. The box it fitted might contain papers or documents valuable as evidence. Considered as part of Mr. Pembroke's estate, it should of course be given into Leroy's charge; but considered as evidence in the Pembroke case, I surely had a right to use it.

Deciding upon my course of action then, I went straight to the Coroner's and asked him for the key. He hesitated at first, but when I gave him the result of my own cogitation on the subject, he said: "You may as well take it, for at least you can find where it belongs. They won't let you open the box, as you are not the executor of the estate, so it can do no harm."

I didn't dispute the point, but I felt a secret conviction that if I found the box to which the key belonged, I should somehow get sight of its contents.

As Mr. Ross seemed inclined to talk about the Pembroke matter I went on to discuss the other clues. He announced his intention of calling in a professional detective, but was waiting for Leroy's return before doing so.

"We've clues enough for a whole gang of burglars," he remarked. "I supposed of course most of these things,"—he was looking over my list,—"would be recognized by some of the family. But since they were not, they would seem to mean something definite in the way of evidence. However, I shall give them all to a detective as soon as possible, and if he can deduce any intruder from outside, and can explain how he effected an entrance, he will be cleverer than any detective in a story-book."

"You have all the clues, I suppose," I said, feeling a distinct sense of dismay at the thought of his detective.

"Yes," he said, opening a drawer of his desk.

With no definite purpose, I examined them, and noted on my list such details as the date and seat numbers on the ticket stubs, the date and wording of the telegram, the initials on the handkerchief and such matters.

"What is this?" I asked, as I noticed an opened envelope addressed to Robert Pembroke.

"That is our newest exhibit," said the Coroner; "it was brought me within the last hour by Inspector Crawford, and it seems to me to eliminate the torn telegram from our case entirely. Read it."

I took the letter from the envelope, and glancing first at the signature saw the name Jonathan Scudder. The letter went on to state that the writer would not be able to call on Mr. Pembroke on Wednesday evening, as he had telegraphed that he would.

"This, then is the mysterious J. S.," I said, "and, as you say it makes it unnecessary for us to trace that clue further."

"Yes," returned Mr. Ross, "but of course it was not a real clue any way, for neither J. S. nor anyone else could enter a chained door."

That everlasting chain! Why do people have chains on their front doors, any way? There was one on our own door, but we never

84

used it, and I wished to Heaven that Janet Pembroke had never used hers! They were supposed to be a safeguard, but in this case this infernal chain was condemning evidence against the woman I loved! That is, it condemned her in the eyes of others, but not in my eyes; nothing could ever do that!

But there was no use of declaring my convictions to the Coroner. He was just as positive that Janet Pembroke was guilty as I was that she was innocent.

However, all question of J. S. was settled. He was Jonathan Scudder, and whether or not he was the man whom Mr. Pembroke had sometimes called John Strong, made no difference to our case. I read the letter again, but it was of little interest and taking the key, which Mr. Ross gave me, I went away.

Somehow, I was not so buoyantly hopeful after my interview with the Coroner as I had been before. The letter from Mr. Scudder did not affect me, it was of no consequence at all, but the Coroner's unshakable conviction of Janet's wrong-doing had made me realize that my own belief was founded not on facts but on my own glorious fancies.

Very well, then, I concluded, I will go to work and get facts that will coincide with my beliefs. Action was better than theorizing, any way, and I went at once to the bank which I had been told carried Mr. Pembroke's account.

But there I was informed that the key I showed was not the property of that bank or any of its departments. Nor could they tell me to what bank or company it did belong. I suspected they might have given me at least a hint of where to look, but as I was unknown to them personally, and they had no knowledge of how I had come by the key, they naturally were conservative on the subject.

I could have explained the situation to them, but I knew it would be useless, as, if I were trying to use the key with fraudulent intent it was just the sort of a story I should have invented. So I turned away, a little despondent, but determined to keep on with my search, if I had to visit every bank in the city.

It was a weary search. After two or three unsuccessful attempts, I took a taxicab and methodically made the rounds of the prominent banks.

But as I met with no success, I concluded finally that such attempt was useless. I suspected that perhaps the bank officials suspected me, and would not give me information. This roused my ire, and as a next step I went to the office of the firm who made the key. As the makers' name was stamped on it I had no difficulty in finding them. Of course they were quite able to tell me for what institution that key had been made, but they were at first unwilling to do so. It was only after a full statement of my case and proofs of my own identity that I gained from them the information that the key had been made for The Sterling Safe Deposit Co.

XIV

MRS. ALTONSTALL

The Sterling Safe Deposit Company! Well, at last I had some definite information! At last I had something to work upon! I went at once to the deposit company, and asked for an interview with the manager. I had difficulty in persuading him to grant my request, but after realizing the gravity of the situation and the significance of the clue, he told me that that key belonged to a safe deposit box rented by a Mrs. Altonstall, who lived on West Fifty-eighth Street.

I looked at my watch. It was almost five o'clock, but I concluded to go at once to call on the lady.

As I went up there in a taxicab, my brain was in a whirl. The key of a safe deposit box, not Mr. Pembroke's own, but belonging to a woman! found in his room, after a crime which it was assumed was committed by a woman!

Who was Mrs. Altonstall? And why should she murder Robert Pembroke? This question opened such a wide field for speculation that it was unanswerable. Had the deed really been done by a woman? And was I, even now, about to verify this?

I felt an uncertainty about proceeding. Ought I not to place the whole matter in the hands of the Coroner? Was I not taking too much upon myself to investigate alone this new evidence?

But, I reasoned, delay might be dangerous. If the Coroner were to postpone until next day an interview with this woman, might she not have already effected her escape? Was it not wiser that I should go there at once, and lose no time in securing any possible information?

At any rate, I went, resolved to take the consequences of my deed, whatever they might be.

The address given me proved to be a large and handsome apartment house. At the office I inquired for Mrs. Altonstall and being informed that she was at home, I sent up my card, for I judged that the most open and straightforward measures were the best.

A moment later I was informed that Mrs. Altonstall would see me, and entering the elevator I went at once to her apartment.

The general effects of grandeur throughout the house and the elegance of Mrs. Altonstall's own room, made me wonder afresh if I could by any possibility be on the track of a criminal. Surely, the criminal classes did not live in a style implying such respectability and aristocracy as these surroundings seemed to indicate. But of course I realized that a woman who could commit murder was not necessarily found among the criminal classes, and indeed, being an exceptional individual, might be looked for in any setting.

But when my hostess entered, and I saw a sweet-faced, middle-aged lady, of gentle manner and gracious mien, walk toward me, I felt the blood rush to my face, and I stood consumed with dismay and confusion.

"Mrs. Altonstall?" I said, conquering my embarrassment.

"Yes," she said, in one of the sweetest voices I ever heard. "This is Mr. Landon? you wanted to see me?"

Surely with such a queen of women as this, frankness and truth were the only lines to follow.

"Yes, Mrs. Altonstall," I said; "I am a lawyer, and I am at present investigating a serious case. In connection with it, there has been found a key, which I have been informed belongs to you. Will you kindly say if this is so?"

As I spoke, I handed her the key. I need not say that at the first glimpse of that serene, gracious face, all thought of her implication in our affair instantly vanished. Presumably, too, the key was not hers, there had been a mistake, somehow.

As she took the key, she looked at me with a bewildered surprise. "Why, yes, Mr. Landon," she said, "this is my key. May I ask where you obtained it?"

I hesitated, for it seemed a terrible thing to tell this queenly lady where her key had been found. And yet the situation was so inexplicable, that I must solve it if possible.

"I will tell you in a moment, Mrs. Altonstall," I said, slowly, "but first I must ask you if you know Mr. Robert Pembroke?"

"Robert Pembroke?" she repeated; "no, I never heard the name. Who is he?"

The unruffled calm and the straightforward gaze that met my own eyes, so frankly, was so convincing of her absolute veracity, that just for an instant the thought flashed through my mind that it might be merely the perfection of acting.

But the next instant I knew better, for no human being could so simulate utter ignorance of a subject, if she had guilty knowledge of it. Moreover, since she knew nothing of Robert Pembroke, I instantly concluded not to tell her of the tragedy, but to inquire further concerning the key.

"Since you do not know him, Mrs. Altonstall, let us not discuss him. Will you tell me how you lost possession of this key, since it is yours?"

"I gave it to my lawyer, Mr. Leroy," she replied. "It was necessary that he should get some of my papers from the Safe

Deposit Company, and it has been arranged that he shall have access to my box on presentation of my key. I am a widow, Mr. Landon, and as I have various financial interests, it is necessary for me frequently to employ the services of a lawyer. Mr. Leroy attends to all such affairs for me."

"Do you mean Mr. Graham Leroy?" I asked, very gravely, for the introduction of his name stirred up all sorts of conjectures.

"Yes," she replied, "he is an able lawyer, as well as a kind friend."

"I'm acquainted with Mr. Leroy," I responded, "and I quite agree with your estimate of him. When did you give him the key, Mrs. Altonstall?"

"About four or five days ago; last Saturday, to be exact. There was no immediate haste about my papers, he was to attend to the matter at his convenience. May I ask where the key was found?"

I disliked extremely to rehearse the details of the case, and I knew it was in no way necessary. Of course the key belonged to this lady; aside from her own word, the bank had told me so. But her question must be answered.

"It was found in the apartment of Mr. Robert Pembroke," I said; but immediately added, as she looked slightly startled, "I think, however, it is a matter of easy explanation. Graham Leroy is also Mr. Pembroke's lawyer, and he must have dropped the key there while calling on Mr. Pembroke."

"Unpardonable carelessness," she said, and I saw that the sweet placid face could assume an expression of indignation upon occasion.

"That, madam, you must say to Mr. Leroy. I am sorry to have troubled you in the matter, and I thank you for your courtesy to me."

"But you will leave my key with me?" she said, as I was about to take leave.

"I think I cannot do that, Mrs. Altonstall," I said, "as it was entrusted to me by official authority. But I promise to return it to Mr. Leroy, which, I trust will be satisfactory to you."

The lady agreed to this, though a little unwillingly, and I went away, newly perplexed at this most recent development.

So then, Graham Leroy had been in possession of this key. So then, he must have left it in Robert Pembroke's bedroom. He would not have done this purposely, of course, therefore he must have dropped it there without knowing it. It was found on Robert Pembroke's bed. Not under the pillow,—the suggestion that it had been under the pillow was mere supposition. It might have been dropped on the bed from the pocket of one leaning over the sleeping man.

But Graham Leroy! the thought was preposterous!

And then again, the old, ever insoluble question,—how could he get in?

But really it was scarcely more impossible to conclude how he got in, than to imagine Graham Leroy getting in at all, except in correct and ordinary fashion.

My brain worked quickly. To be sure, he might have dropped the key in that room when calling there, as he did, on Tuesday night. But I had asked Charlotte when Mr. Pembroke's bedroom had last been swept, and she had told me that she had swept it Wednesday morning, and had then emptied the waste basket. This had seemed to me to prove that all the clues I had found, had been brought into the room after that sweeping. But again, the key being found in the bed it had nothing to do with the sweeping of the room. However, Charlotte could not have made up the bed without seeing the key, so the only possible deduction was that Mrs. Altonstall's key had been left in Robert Pembroke's room after noon of Wednesday, the day he was murdered!

It was all too much for me! I had undertaken to trace the clues that I had myself found, but if they were to lead me to such extraordinary discoveries as this, I felt I must appeal to more practical detective talent.

But Leroy or not, at any rate it turned the tide of suspicion away from Janet. This was joy enough, of itself, to compensate for any horrible revelation that might come in the future concerning Leroy or anyone else.

Somewhere in the back of my brain two dreadful words that the Coroner had used were hammering for admittance. These were connivance and complicity; if Leroy entered the apartment on Wednesday night at any hour he was let in by either Janet or Charlotte.

At that moment I realized the truth of the line, "that way madness lies."

I pushed the thought from my mind with all my will power, and hastening my steps, for I had walked from Fifty-eighth Street, I went rapidly homeward.

I reached home about six o'clock, and found that George Lawrence was there, and that Laura had invited him to stay to dinner. I was pleased at this, for I hoped that by the casual conversation at table I could learn something of Mr. Pembroke's past life and acquaintances.

I concluded to say nothing about my discoveries of the

afternoon, but to advise them of my decision to continue my search for a real criminal; a housebreaker or burglar, who could have committed the crime for the money, which he stole, and who must have contrived some way to get in through a window.

During dinner, although Laura endeavored to keep away from the all-engrossing subject, which she disapproved of as table conversation, I gave a slight outline of the effort I intended to make.

George Lawrence seemed greatly pleased with my ideas. He agreed that there must be some one, somewhere, besides himself and Janet who could be shown to have a motive, and he offered to assist me in looking over his uncle's private papers for some letter or other evidence which might indicate this.

"Simply to make a statement of the case, but for no other reason," said George, "I will agree with you that the facts, as known, seem to implicate Janet. But as she is utterly incapable of such a thing, and as the idea of Charlotte being involved in the matter is absurd, the criminal must be somebody else, and we must find him or her. I say 'him or her' because the inspector declares that the hat-pin indicates a woman's deed, and, as we are utterly at sea regarding the individuality of the criminal, we are, I think, justified in assuming either sex. It is, of course, not beyond the bounds of possibility that Uncle Robert had a feminine enemy."

"Once we can establish a motive," I said, "we shall have something to work upon in our hunt for evidence."

"And yet motive isn't everything," said Lawrence, with a grim smile; "for if Janet had a motive, as you say, an equal one must be attributed to me, as I am an equal inheritor of Uncle Robert's fortune."

I looked wonderingly at the young man. "The motive attributed to Miss Pembroke," I said "would probably not be her desire for inheritance, so much as the desperate difficulties attending her life with her uncle."

This seemed to surprise Lawrence, but he only said carelessly: "It doesn't matter what motive they assign to Janet, for she didn't have any motive, and she didn't do the deed. But, for the moment, I'm speaking not of facts or even possibilities, but of contingencies which might arise. It might be claimed that I had a motive, from the mere fact that I am one of my uncle's heirs."

"But you couldn't get in, George," said Janet quickly. "Your latch-key was of no use when the chain was on."

"That's true enough, Janet, and we all know it; but, as I say, we're speaking of a hypothetical case. And you know, if we're going to hunt for some other person with a motive, we're bound to admit that he got into the apartment somehow. Therefore, to eliminate the

91

possibility of being myself a suspect, I'll merely state, as a matter of fact, that my alibi is perfect. I can prove, should it be necessary, that I was far away from Sixty-second Street at the time of Uncle Robert's death, and can account for my time all through the night."

I liked Lawrence's way of putting these things, and began to think his clear-headed views on the matter would be of assistance to me, even though he had no taste or talent for detective work.

"Just what is an alibi?" asked Janet, with a perplexed air.

"It means," I answered, "proof by witnesses of a person's whereabouts at a given time."

"Oh!" said Janet. "And where were you last night, George?"

Lawrence smiled as he answered: "I'm not in the witness box now, Janet, but I don't mind telling you that I dined and spent the evening at the Warings'."

"Oh, did you?" cried Janet. "And you took Milly to a matinée in the afternoon. I know, because she told me about it before. You're getting awfully fond of her, aren't you, George?"

"Yes, I like Miss Waring extremely," said Lawrence, and though he spoke as if he meant it, a certain sadness came into his eyes, and I suspected that Miss Waring did not reciprocate his regard.

But though the young man seemed suddenly distrait, and did not attempt to continue our previous conversation, Janet, on the contrary had brightened up wonderfully. Being in a mood for making inferences, I deduced that George Lawrence was more interested in Miss Waring than Janet desired him to be, and that she was pleased rather than otherwise at George's lack of enthusiasm about the lady. Thereupon the sudden fear that Janet was in love with her cousin assailed me. This aroused what was of course an unreasonable jealousy on my part, for I had not the slightest actual foundation on which to rest the hopes I was rapidly building. I eagerly watched the two cousins after that, to discover if there was anything more than cousinly affection on either side.

XV

WHO IS J. S.?

Whatever the cause, Janet's spirits were undeniably lightened.

"I wish I could help," she said. "Here is our problem: to find somebody who wanted to kill Uncle Robert, and who was able to get into the apartment and do so."

"That's the case in a nutshell," declared George; "but I confess I don't know which way to start."

Although I had made up my mind not to refer to the letter from Jonathan Scudder, which Crawford had shown me, yet I thought I would introduce the subject of J. S. and see if Janet would volunteer any information regarding the letter.

So, since both cousins had declared their willingness to consider the problem, I said: "As you say you don't know which way to start, Mr. Lawrence, suppose we take up the clue of the torn telegram. Do you think that J. S. who sent that message might have kept his appointment, and come last night, although no one knew it?"

"How could he get in?" asked Lawrence.

"That remains to be explained; but just granting for a moment that he did get in, why not turn our attention to discovering who he is and what his errand was?"

"All right," agreed Lawrence, "but how shall we set about it? We know nothing of the man, not even his real name."

"What do you think, Miss Pembroke?" I asked, turning to Janet; "do you think it would be possible for us to learn the real name of J. S.?"

The girl looked at me with troubled eyes, but the expression of her mouth denoted determination. Even before she spoke, I knew that she was not going to tell of the letter she had read that morning. The letter was addressed to her uncle, but it had been opened. The reasonable explanation of this was that it had come in that morning's mail, as indeed its postmark proved, and that Janet had opened and read it; this latter supposition being probable, because the letter had been found in her room. To be sure after the death of her uncle, she was next in charge of the household affairs, but it would have been more commendable of her to have given her uncle's unopened mail to his lawyer or to some one in charge of his estate.

When she spoke, as I had fully expected, she made no reference to the letter.

"As I have told you," she said slowly, "my uncle often used to speak of J. S., and when we asked him who it was, he said John Strong."

"But we know he didn't mean it," said Lawrence; "and also, Mr. Landon, although I do not know his real name, I'm positive that J. S. is the man who was my uncle's business partner many years ago. In fact my uncle has said to me that this partner thought that half of Uncle Robert's fortune should be given to him, or bequeathed to him by will. My uncle said he had no intention of doing this, but I gathered from his remarks on the subject, that his partner was continually making fresh efforts to obtain some of my uncle's money."

"Then, in view of all this," I said, "is there not at least reason to look up this J. S. who sent the telegram, and see if he might not be the man whom your uncle called John Strong?"

I looked directly at Janet as I said this, and though she returned my gaze at first, her eyes fell before my questioning glance, and her voice trembled ever so little as she said; "yes, let us do that."

"It is a very good idea," broke in sister Laura, who was quick of decision and who rarely hesitated to express her opinions. "This John Strong may have been delayed, and reached the apartment very late at night. Then there may have been a stormy interview, and, unable to get what he wanted from Mr. Pembroke, John Strong may have killed the old gentleman, taken the money that is missing from the desk and gone away."

"Sister dear," I said, "your theory is fairly plausible. If you don't mind I'll ask you to elucidate it a little further. Just how did John Strong get into Mr. Pembroke's apartment?"

"Why," returned Laura, "Mr. Pembroke was expecting him, and as it was late, and the others were in bed, he got up and let the man in himself."

"Yes; I understand," I went on; "and now, then, after this wicked Mr. Strong had committed his dreadful deed, who let him out, and put the chain on the door?"

There was a dead silence. I had chosen my words most unfortunately. I had spoken rather quizzically, only with the intention of showing Laura how absurd her idea was; but my final question, instead of merely confuting her theory, had also suggested a dreadful possibility! For if anybody had put the chain on after the departure of the mythical Mr. Strong, it must necessarily have been one of the two living occupants of the apartment!

Janet turned white to her very lips, and as a consequence, even

94

more dreadful thoughts flashed into my mind. She had read a letter that day from the man who had sent the telegram. There was practically no doubt of that. When I had asked her concerning this man just now, though she had not denied, yet she had not admitted the knowledge which she must have possessed. And now when the faintest hint was breathed of a possible complicity of some one in the apartment with this mysterious J. S., Janet was so agitated as to turn pale and almost quiver with apprehension!

I was strongly tempted to tell of the letter the Inspector had shown me, but I could not bring myself to do so, for far deeper than my interest in the case was my interest in this girl; and if that letter must be brought forward against her, it would have to be done by some one else and not by me. My evidence about the chain on the door had already wrought irremediable damage, and hereafter my efforts should be devoted to showing evidence that should prove Janet Pembroke innocent, and not of a sort which should make her seem to be guilty!

"How would you advise trying to find this man?" asked George Lawrence, after a somewhat awkward pause; "the address on the telegram was East Lynnwood, but it would be difficult, even with a directory or census report to find a name of which we know only the initials."

"Yes," agreed Laura, "there are doubtless men in East Lynnwood whose initials are J. S. Indeed, I should say those are perhaps the most common initials of all. You see, so many men's names begin with J."

"And it may not be a man at all," suggested Lawrence. "Women's names often begin with J,—like Janet for instance."

"But my initials are not J. S.," returned his cousin, "and besides, I didn't telegraph to uncle Robert."

Again the girl surprised me, for she spoke in a light tone, as if almost amused at the idea.

"But it might have been a woman," she went on, "which would explain the hat-pin."

I was thoroughly perplexed at Miss Pembroke's words. She knew the J. S. of the telegram was the Jonathan Scudder of the letter. She knew therefore that J. S. was not a woman. Why was she so disingenuous? Was she shielding J. S., and did she know far more about the tragedy than I had supposed? At any rate, I could see she was determined not to tell of the letter she had read, and I was determined that if I should ask her concerning it, it would be when alone with her, for I would not subject her to possible humiliation before others.

"We certainly can do nothing in the matter without knowing

95

more of J. S. than we do now," I said, with an air of dropping the subject; "and I doubt, even if we should find him, that it would help us to discover the mystery."

"I don't believe it will ever be discovered," said Laura. "It looks to me like one of those mysteries that are never solved. For whoever it was that was clever enough to get into that house, when there wasn't any way to get in, would also be clever enough to evade detection."

George and Janet both looked at Laura as if startled by her remark. The fact that they were startled startled me. If they had known the clever individual whom Laura merely imagined, they couldn't have acted differently. But all this muddle of impressions on my mind really led to nothing. "If I'm going to do any detecting," I said to myself severely, "it's time I set about it, and not depend on guessing what people may mean by the expressions on their faces—especially faces capable of such ambiguous expressions as the two before me."

Determined, therefore, to lead the conversation into channels that would at least put me in the way of learning some facts about the previous life of the Pembrokes and of George Lawrence, I spoke generally of ways and means of living in New York. I learned that Janet had the tastes and inclinations of a society girl, but that, owing to her uncle's restrictions, she had been able only slightly to gratify these inclinations. She was fond of concerts and theatres, of going shopping and calling, and yet had never been allowed the money or the freedom to pursue these pleasures. My heart sank as I realized how everything the girl said would tell against her should she ever be called to the witness box.

Young Lawrence, it seemed, had similar social tastes, but even when he lived with the Pembrokes had been more free to go and come than his cousin. And, of course, since he had lived alone he was entirely his own master. He was a member of various clubs, and seemed to be fond of card-playing and billiards, in moderation. I also learned, though, I think, through an inadvertence, that he dabbled a little in Wall Street. It seemed surprising that a young artist could support himself in comfortable bachelor quarters and still have money left with which to speculate. This would not be in his favor, had there been a shadow of suspicion against him; but there could be no such suspicion, for even with his latch-key he could not get in at the door. He could hardly be taken for a professional housebreaker; and, besides, he was prepared to prove an alibi. I had little faith in this mythical personage we had built up with a motive and an opportunity, and as I reasoned round and round in a circle I was always confronted by the terrifying fact that a disinterested judge would suspect Janet and that, were I disinterested, I should suspect her myself. And so the reasoning went on in my excited brain, till I felt that I must go for a long walk in the cool night air as the only means of regaining my own clearness of vision.

Soon after dinner, then, I announced my intention of going out.

Lawrence said that he would spend some hours looking over his late uncle's papers, and Laura declared that she would tuck Miss Pembroke in bed early for a good night's rest.

I started out by myself, and, swinging into Broadway, I turned and walked rapidly downtown. This was my custom when I had serious matters to think of. The crowded brightness of the street always seemed to stimulate my brain, while it quieted my nerves. I hadn't gone a dozen blocks before I had come to two or three different conclusions, right or wrong though they may have been.

The first of these was a conviction that Janet felt more than a cousinly interest in George Lawrence. But this I also concluded might be caused by one of two things; it might be either a romantic attachment or Janet might suspect her cousin to be guilty of her uncle's death. If the first were true, Janet might have been in league with George and might have opened the door for him the night before. I was facing the thing squarely now, and laying aside any of my own prejudices or beliefs, while I considered mere possibilities.

If, on the other hand, Janet suspected George, without real knowledge, this fact of course left Janet herself free of all suspicion. While I couldn't believe that the two had connived at their uncle's death, still less could I believe that Janet had done the deed herself. Therefore, I must face all the possibilities, and even endeavor to imagine more than I had yet thought of.

But the more I considered imaginary conditions, the more they seemed to me ridiculous and untenable. George was not in the apartment; Janet was. George was not at the mercy of his uncle's brutal temper; Janet was. George did not want money and freedom to pursue his chosen ways of life; Janet did.

Much as I liked George, I would gladly have cast the weight of suspicion on him instead of on Janet, had I but been able to do so.

I had never before felt so utterly at the end of my resources. There was no one to suspect, other than those already mentioned, and no place to look for new evidence. Either the talent I had always thought I possessed for detective work was non-existent, or else there was not enough for me to work upon.

But I had traced two clues. The telegram, though it had not implicated J. S. had pointed, indirectly, in Janet's direction. The key, though still mysterious, at least gave a hint of Leroy, and perhaps, in complicity, Janet.

I made these statements frankly to myself, because since I was going to fight her battle, I wanted to know at the outset what I had to fight against.

Having started on my investigation, I was eager to continue the quest I felt, if damaging evidence must be found, I would rather find it myself, than be told of it by some conceited, unsympathetic detective.

But there was little I could do by way of investigation in the evening. However, as I passed through the theatre district, I bethought me of the ticket stubs. Though well aware it was but a wild goose chase, I turned my steps toward the National Theatre. As the program was fairly well along, there was not a crowd at the box office, and I had no difficulty in engaging the blithe young man at the window in conversation. I had not the ticket stubs with me, but I had a memorandum of their dates, and though it sounded absurd even to myself, I made inquiry concerning them.

"House sold out, I suppose?" I said, carelessly, to the face at the window.

"Just about. Want a poor seat?"

"No; I'll wait till some other night. Is it sold out every night?"

"Just about."

"Was it sold out the night of October sixteenth?"

"Sure! that was in one of our big weeks! Great program on then. Why?"

"I don't suppose you could tell me who bought seats one and three in row G, that night?"

"I should say not! do you s'pose I'm a human chart? What's the game?"

"Detective work," I said, casually, thinking he would be less impressed if I did not seem too much interested. "I suppose you can't think of any way that I could find out who bought those seats for that night?"

"Well, no, I can't; unless you might advertise."

"Advertise! how?"

"Why put in a personal, asking for the fellows that had those seats."

"But they wouldn't reply; they don't want to be caught."

"Sure, that's so! well, I'll tell you. Put your personal in and ask the fellows who sat behind those seats to communicate with you. Then you can find out something about your party, may be."

"Young man," I said, heartily, "that's a really brilliant idea! I shall act upon it, and I'm much obliged to you."

98

I offered him a material proof of my gratitude for his suggestion, which he accepted with pleasure, and I went straight away to a newspaper office. This scheme might amount to nothing at all, but on the other hand, it certainly could do no harm.

I inserted a personal notice in the paper, asking that the holders of the seats near one and three G on the night of October sixteenth should communicate with me. I mentioned the numbers of the seats not only behind the mysterious numbers, but in front of them as well, and also at the side. I had little hope that this venture would bring any worth-while result, but there was a chance that it might, and action of any sort was better than doing nothing.

After leaving the newspaper office, I continued my walk, hoping, by deep thought to arrive at some conclusion, or at least to think of some new direction in which to look. But the farther I walked, and the more I thought, the more desperate the situation became. Clear thought and logical inference led only in one direction; and that was toward Janet Pembroke. To lead suspicion away from her, could only be done by dwelling on the thought of my love for her. In spite of her mysterious ways, perhaps because of them, my love for her was fast developing into a mad infatuation, beyond logic and beyond reason. But it was a power, and a power, I vowed, that should yet conquer logic and reason,—aye, even evidence and proof of any wrong-doing on the part of my goddess!

Notwithstanding appearances, notwithstanding Janet's own inexplicable words and deeds, I believed her entirely innocent, and I would prove it to the world.

Yet I knew that I based my belief in her innocence on that one fleeting moment, when she had looked at me with tenderness in her brown eyes, and with truth stamped indelibly upon her beautiful face.

Was that too brief a moment, too uncertain a bond to be depended upon?

XVI

LEROY ARRIVES ON THE SCENE

When I reached home Lawrence had left, Miss Pembroke had retired, and Laura was in the library, waiting for me.

"It doesn't seem possible," she said, as I flung off my coat and threw myself into an easy chair, "that so much could have happened in one day. Only think, Otis, when we arose this morning we didn't know Miss Pembroke to speak to, and now she is asleep in our guest room!"

"Where is Charlotte?" I said.

"She wanted to go to spend the night with some friends, so I let her go. We are responsible, you know, for her appearance if called for, and I know the girl well enough to know she'll never get very far away from her beloved Miss Janet."

"Have you questioned Charlotte at all?"

"Yes; and what do you think Otis? She believes that Miss Pembroke killed her uncle!"

"Did she say so?"

"Not in so many words; indeed, she scarcely owned up to it. But you know colored people are as transparent as children, and by talking in a roundabout way I discovered that she suspects Janet, only because she can't see any other solution of the mystery. She doesn't seem to blame her at all, and even seems to think Janet justified in putting the old man out of the way."

"Of course she has no intelligence in the matter," I said; "but don't you see, Laura, that if she suspects Janet, but really knows nothing about it, that proves Charlotte herself absolutely innocent even of complicity?"

"So it does, Otis. How clever you are to see that!"

"Clever!" I said, somewhat bitterly. "I'm not clever at all. I may be a lawyer, but I'm no detective."

"Why don't you employ a detective, then?"

"It isn't my place to do so. But I feel sure that a professional detective, from the clues we have, could find the murderer at once."

"Well, it wouldn't be Janet Pembroke," said Laura, with conviction. "I've been alone with that girl most of the evening, and she's no more guilty than I am. But, Otis, she does know more than she has told. She either knows something or suspects something that she is keeping secret."

100

"I have thought that, too. And, as her counsel, she ought to be perfectly frank with me."

"But isn't there a law or something," asked Laura, "that people are not obliged to say anything that may incriminate themselves?"

"But you don't think her a criminal," I said quickly.

"No," said Laura, with some hesitation; "but she is so queer in some ways, I can't make her out. Mr. Lawrence stayed here chatting some time after you left, and once or twice I thought Janet suspected him; and then, again, she said something that showed me positively that she didn't."

"There it is again, Laura: if Janet suspects George, she can't be guilty herself."

"That's so," said Laura, her face brightening. "But then," she added, "they both may know something about it."

Ah, this was my own fear! "Laura," I said suddenly, "do you think those two cousins are in love with each other?"

"Not a bit of it," said Laura decidedly. "Mr. Lawrence is very much interested in Miss Millicent Waring, though I don't know that he is really in love with her. But I think he is rather piqued by her indifference. He seems to have a loyal fondness for Janet, but nothing more than would be expected from a good first-class cousin."

"And she?" I asked, trying hard not to appear self-conscious.

"Oh, she cares for George in the same way. He's her only relative now, you know. But she told me herself she had never cared especially for any man. She's peculiar, you know, Otis; but I do think she shows a great deal of interest in you."

"Do you really?" I exclaimed, looking up to find my sister smiling at me in a mischievous fashion.

"Oh, you dear old goose!" she cried. "Do you suppose I can't see that you're already over head and ears in love with Janet Pembroke, and have been ever since the first day we came into the Hammersleigh?"

"By Jove! that's so," I cried. "Laura, you know more about my affairs than I do. I thought my affection for that girl dated from this morning, but I see now you are right. I have loved her from the first moment I saw her."

"And you can win her, if you go about it right," said my sister, with her little air of worldly wisdom that always amused me.

"I hope so," I said fervently. "As soon as this dreadful affair is finished up, and Janet has decided upon her temporary home, I think we too want to get away from this place."

"Yes," said Laura, with a sigh; "I hate to move, but I'd hate worse to stay here."

In response to the urgent summons Leroy came back to New York the next morning.

From his office he telephoned to Janet immediately upon his return, saying that he would come up to see her in the afternoon, and asking that George Lawrence should also be present.

As Janet was now staying with us, the interview was held in our apartment. Although Mr. Pembroke's body had been removed to a mortuary establishment, Janet could not bear the thought of going back to her own rooms, and moreover, the girl was very glad to remain under the cheering influences of Laura's kindness and friendliness. And so, as Laura insisted upon it, Janet directed Mr. Leroy to come up that afternoon.

This being arranged, Laura also telephoned me at my office, and I went home in ample time to receive our caller.

As Miss Pembroke's lawyer I had, of course, a right to be present, and as George Lawrence was there too, it seemed more like an official interview than a social call.

Leroy came in, looking exceedingly handsome and attractive. Indeed, I had forgotten what an unusually good-looking man he was. He had that combination of dark eyes and hair slightly silvered at the temples, which is so effective in middle age.

Though not at all effusive in his manner, he seemed deeply moved, and greeted Janet with an air of gentle sympathy. His manner, however, did not meet a response in kind. Janet's air was cold and haughty and she merely gave him her finger tips, as if the very touch of his hand were distasteful to her.

George Lawrence was a little more cordial in his reception of the lawyer, but it was plain to be seen that neither of the cousins felt very friendly toward him.

Mr. Leroy acknowledged courteously his introduction to Laura and myself, and then he requested to be told the details of the tragedy.

He listened attentively while we told him all about it, now and then asking a question, but expressing no opinions. His face grew very grave, indeed to me it seemed almost sinister, and a little mysterious.

We had not yet finished relating the case, when our door-bell rang and Mr. Buckner was announced.

Buckner was the District Attorney, and after receiving the Coroner's report he had come to make some further inquiries.

I had never seen the man before, as I rarely had to do with a criminal case, but I liked his attitude and manner at once. He was exceedingly straightforward and business-like. He asked questions and conducted his inquiries as if it were merely a continuation of the inquest.

He had of course learned from the coroner all that he knew about the case, and now he seemed to hope and expect that he would get new evidence from Leroy.

However, Graham Leroy was not a satisfactory person to get evidence from. He answered the District Attorney's questions, directly and concisely, but he gave little or no information of any importance.

Leroy had not seemed especially interested in hearing of the clues which I had collected from Mr. Pembroke's bedroom, but after a time I concluded to try the effect of showing him the key which I had in my pocket.

"Good Heavens!" he exclaimed, with a start, "where did you get that?"

The result of my sudden move was all I could have desired. Leroy's calm was shaken at last; his interest was aroused, and the strange expression that showed on his saturnine face proved that he was greatly agitated at the sight of that key. It seemed to me that fear possessed him, or that at any rate he was startled by some unpleasant thought.

The District Attorney, who had been apprised by the Coroner of my tracing of the key, turned to Leroy with a hint of accusation in his manner.

"You recognize that key, Mr. Leroy?" he said.

"I do," returned Leroy, and though he spoke in quiet tones, he had difficulty in concealing his agitation.

"Is it yours?"

"It is not mine, but it was in my possession."

"Whose is it?"

"It belongs to Mrs. Altonstall, a client of mine. She gave it to me, to get some papers for her from a safety deposit box."

"And you lost it?"

"I did."

"When did you have it last, to your knowledge?"

"I had it on Wednesday. I went to Utica, Wednesday night, and next morning I missed the key. I concluded that I must have left it at my office, but when I returned there I could not find it, and I felt considerable alarm, for one does not like to lose the key of a client's box."

"No," said Mr. Buckner, grimly; "it is not a good thing to do. And where do you think you lost it?"

"I've no idea; but as it was in my pocket, and I must have pulled it out unintentionally, and dropped it unknowingly, it may have happened in the train or on the street or anywhere. Where was it found?"

"This is the key of which we told you; the key that was found in Mr. Pembroke's bed yesterday morning."

"What! Impossible!" cried Leroy and his face turned white and his dark eyes fairly glared. "How could Robert Pembroke have come into possession of that key?"

"We don't assume, Mr. Leroy, that Mr. Pembroke ever had this key in his possession. As it was found in the bed, not under the pillow, but beside the body of the dead man, we think it seems to indicate at least a possibility that it was dropped there by the murderer as he leaned over his victim."

This came so near to being a direct accusation, that I fully expected Leroy to exclaim with anger. But instead, though his face grew even whiter than before, he said very quietly: "Am I to understand that as an implication that I may be guilty of this crime?"

Though uttered in low even tones, the words expressed horror at the thought.

"You are to understand," replied Mr. Buckner, "that we ask you for a frank and honest explanation of how your key, or rather your client's key, happened to be where it was found."

"I cannot explain it," said Leroy, and now he had entirely controlled his agitation, and his face was like an impassive marble mask.

"You cannot or you will not?"

"I cannot. I have not the remotest idea where I lost that key, but by no possibility could I have lost it in Mr. Pembroke's bedroom, because I was not there."

"When were you last in Mr. Pembroke's room?"

"I was there Tuesday evening, and I may possibly have dropped the key there then."

"But you said you remembered having it Wednesday morning."

"I might be mistaken about that; perhaps it was Tuesday morning that I positively remember having it."

Clearly Leroy was floundering. His words were hesitating, and though it was evident that his brain was working quickly, I felt sure he was trying to conceal his thoughts, and not express them.

"Supposing then that you may have dropped this key in Mr. Pembroke's bedroom when you were calling on him Tuesday evening, you would not be likely to have dropped it in the bed, would you?"

"Certainly not. I saw Mr. Pembroke in his room only a few

moments, after having already made a longer call in the drawing-room."

The involuntary glance which Leroy shot at Janet and the color which flamed suddenly in the girl's face, left me in no doubt as to the purport of the call he had made in the drawing-room on Tuesday evening. I knew as well as if I had been told, that he had been asking Janet to marry him; I knew that his interview with Mr. Pembroke afterward had probably related to the same subject; and though I was glad that his suit had not been successful, yet I felt jealous of the whole episode. However, I had no time then to indulge in thoughts of romance, for the District Attorney was mercilessly pinning Leroy down to an exact account of himself.

"Had the bed been turned down for the night, when you were in Mr. Pembroke's room on Tuesday evening?"

"I didn't notice especially, but I have an indistinct impression that the covers had been turned back."

"In that case it would have been possible for you to drop the key in the bed without knowing it, but very far from probable. Did you lean over the bed for any purpose?"

"No; of course I did not. But perhaps if I did drop the key in the room, and Mr. Pembroke found it, knowing it to be a valuable key, he may have put it under his pillow, for safety's sake."

"That again is possible; but improbable that he would have done it two nights, both Tuesday and Wednesday nights! Moreover, Mr. Leroy, you said at first that you were sure you had the key Wednesday morning. And not until you inferred that you were suspected of implication in this affair, did you say that it might have been Tuesday morning you had it. Now, can you not speak positively on that point?"

Leroy hesitated. Though his face rarely showed what was passing in his mind, yet though at this moment no one who saw him could doubt that the man was going through a fearful mental struggle. Indeed, he sat silent for so long, that I began to wonder whether he intended to answer the question or not. Lines formed across his brow and his stern lips fastened themselves in a straight line. He looked first at Janet and then at George, with a piercing gaze. Finally he shook his head with a sudden quick gesture, as if flinging off a temptation to prevaricate, which was almost too strong to be resisted.

"I can speak positively," he said, and the words seemed to be fairly forced from him. "I had that key last to my knowledge on Wednesday morning, when I made use of it at the Sterling Safety Deposit Company."

XVII

CAN LEROY BE GUILTY?

It was as if a bomb had burst. We all sat appalled, for at the first thought it seemed as if this admission proclaimed Graham Leroy a guilty man. The picture flashed into my mind. This strong man, capable I felt sure, of the whole range of elemental passions, killing, for some reason unknown to me, his client, who was equally capable of rage and angry passion. I seemed to see him bending over his victim, and inadvertently dropping the tell-tale key from his pocket. But I think it was an effect of the dramatic situation that conjured up this picture in my mind, for it was immediately dispelled as Janet's voice broke on the tense silence.

"I cannot fail to see the trend of your implications, Mr. Buckner," she said, and her tones were haughty, and even supercilious; "I suppose you are daring to insinuate that Mr. Leroy might have been in my uncle's room on Wednesday night, late. But let me remind you that I myself put the chain on the door at eleven o'clock, after which it was impossible for Mr. Leroy to enter."

The old argument: "How could he get in?"

And though this argument seemed to turn suspicion toward Janet, it did not in the least do so to my mind.

Of course, I had no answer to the question, but that did not change my conviction that Janet was innocent. Could Leroy be guilty? I didn't know, and I didn't much care, if only suspicion could be turned away from Janet!

It was by an effort that I brought my attention back to the conversation going on.

"Will you tell me, Mr. Leroy, where you were on Wednesday night?" went on the District Attorney, making no recognition of Janet's speech beyond a slight bow in her direction.

"I went to Utica," answered Leroy.

"At what time?"

Again there was a lengthy interval of silence, and then Leroy said, in a low voice, "Rather late in the evening."

"On what train?"

"On a late train."

"The midnight train?"

"Yes;" the answer was fairly blurted out as if in utter exasperation.

Although the rest of his hearers started at the realization of all that this implied, Mr. Buckner proceeded quietly. "Where were you between eleven and twelve o'clock, on Wednesday night?"

"I refuse to say."

"I think I must insist upon an answer, Mr. Leroy. Were you at the station long before train time?"

"No."

"You reached the station then but a short time before the train left?"

"That is right."

"Did you go directly from your home to the station?"

"Perhaps not directly, but I made no stop on the way."

"What did you do then, since you say you did not go directly?"

"I walked about the streets."

"Why did you do this?"

"Partly for the exercise, and partly because I preferred not to reach the station until about time for my train to leave."

"And did your walking about the streets bring you anywhere near this locality?"

"That I refuse to answer."

"But you must answer, Mr. Leroy."

"Not if it incriminates myself."

"Then your refusal to answer is the same as affirmative. I shall assume that you were in this locality between eleven and twelve o'clock on Wednesday night."

"What if he was?" broke in Janet; "no matter how much he was in this locality, he couldn't get into our apartment, and so it has not the slightest bearing on the case!"

"That is so," said George Lawrence; "unless it can be proved that Mr. Leroy was able to enter through a locked and chained door, I think it is none of our business where he may have been at the time the crime was committed."

"You're all working from the wrong end," said Leroy, suddenly. "Of course the murder was committed by some professional burglar, who effected his entrance in some way unknown to us. Forget, for a moment, the question of how he got in, and turn your energies to finding some clever and expert housebreaker who is at large."

"What could be the motive of a professional burglar?" said Mr. Buckner.

"The robbery of the money," I broke in eagerly, delighted that Leroy should have started suspicion of this sort.

"Can you tell us anything regarding a large sum of money which it is assumed Mr. Pembroke had in his possession the night he was killed?" Mr. Buckner asked of Leroy.

"I can tell you that I took him a large sum of money,—ten thousand dollars,—on Tuesday evening.

"He had asked you to do this?"

"He had; giving the reason that he wished to pay it to some man who was coming to get it, and who wanted cash."

"J. S.!" I said, involuntarily.

"That's the murderer!" declared Laura. "I've suspected that J. S. from the very beginning. Why don't you look him up, Mr. Buckner, if you want to find the criminal?"

"All in good time, Mrs. Mulford," the district attorney answered, but I knew that he had seen the letter which the Coroner had shown me, stating that J. S. would not come on Wednesday evening as he had telegraphed. Still, if J. S. had come, and with evil intent, the letter might have been a blind. But again, if J. S. had come for money, and had received it, why should he kill Mr. Pembroke? Truly, there was no logical direction in which to look, save toward Janet, and that way I declined to look.

Mr. Buckner did not seem inclined to ask any more definite questions. I concluded he wished to take time to think the matter over by himself.

"It seems to me this way," he said; "we have a great many clues to work from, and until they're traced to more definite conclusions we are unable to attach suspicion to anyone. We know that Mr. Pembroke was killed at or about midnight. We know the apartment was securely locked and fastened at that time. We must assume, therefore, that whoever did the deed could not get into the house between eleven and twelve,—he must have been in the house, therefore, before the door was chained."

"If by that you mean Miss Pembroke," burst out George Lawrence, angrily, "I'll have you know——"

"I don't necessarily mean Miss Pembroke," said Mr. Buckner, but he said it so gravely, that I knew his suspicions, notwithstanding Leroy and his key, were in Janet's direction. "I am thinking just now of the possibility of an intruder who might have come in much earlier, and secreted himself in the house until midnight."

"Then he must have stayed in the house until morning," said Lawrence.

"He might have done so," agreed Mr. Buckner.

"But it is incredible," said Leroy, "that the burglar would have remained after the deed was done. Why would he not take off the chain and go away as silently as he came?"

"It might be," said Mr. Buckner, thoughtfully, "that he meant to cast suspicion upon the inmates of the house themselves."

So he did hark back to Janet after all! He meant us to

understand that he thought the crime was committed either by Janet, or by somebody who planned to throw suspicion on Janet. Either theory seemed to me absurd.

I was glad when Mr. Buckner at last took his departure. He was certainly at sea regarding the matter. He suspected Janet, to be sure; but he also had doubts concerning the entire innocence of Graham Leroy. And surely that key was a bit of incriminating evidence, if ever there were such a thing.

And yet, when it came to a question of evidence, what could be more incriminating than that chained door as a proof against Janet? And so Mr. Buckner went away leaving the rest of us to discuss the new turn events had taken.

It must have been the result of Mr. Buckner's implied accusation of Leroy that gave us all a feeling of loyalty and helpfulness toward the man. I don't think anyone present suspected him of crime. But the key matter was inexplicable, and too, Leroy's manner and speech had not been frank or ingenuous. If he really had been in Robert Pembroke's bedroom on Wednesday night, he could not have acted differently under the fire of Mr. Buckner's questions. And though each of us, I felt sure, was considering the possible explanation of the key, yet it was difficult to speak of it without embarrassment.

But Leroy himself introduced the subject.

"Confounded queer about that key," he said, but he said it thoughtfully, more as if talking to himself than to us.

"It is queer," I said, eagerly taking up the subject; "if you had it Wednesday morning, and it was found in Mr. Pembroke's room Thursday morning, there must be an explanation somewhere."

"Yes; there must;" and Graham Leroy's lips closed as if in a sudden determination to say nothing more about that matter.

"Can't you suggest any explanation?" asked George Lawrence.

"No, I can't," and the decision in Leroy's tones forbade any further reference to the key. "But I am here now," he went on, "to read to you, Mr. Lawrence, and to you, Miss Pembroke, the will of your late uncle. Except for a few minor bequests, you two are equal heirs. Mr. Lawrence is executor, and therefore I will conduct the legal formalities with him, and I need not trouble Miss Pembroke with such matters. Of course, it goes without saying that anything I can do in the investigation of this awful tragedy will be done. Of course, you will want legal advice Miss Pembroke, since the authorities seem to consider you under surveillance."

I waited a moment, to give Janet opportunity to speak first concerning me, and she did so. Her beautiful face was pale, but her dark eyes flashed, as she said: "I feel sure I shall need legal counsel, Mr. Leroy, and therefore I have retained Mr. Landon as my lawyer."

Graham Leroy was astounded. I could read that, in the sudden start he gave, and the half-breathed exclamation which he suppressed. But in a moment, he recovered his poise, and spoke with a cold dignity. "I suppose, Janet, you had some good reason for preferring Mr. Landon's services to my own."

"I had," returned Janet, in tones as icy as his own; "also, Mr. Landon and Mrs. Mulford have been exceedingly kind to me, and I am sure whatever emergency may arise, if the case is brought to trial, Mr. Landon will use his best efforts in my behalf."

If Leroy was angry at her preferring me to himself, he lost sight of it for the moment, in the shock given him by Janet's words.

"The case brought to trial!" he exclaimed. "Why, there is no case as yet. What do you mean?"

Janet looked at him steadily. "I may be tried," she said, "for the murder of my Uncle Robert."

"What nonsense!" cried George Lawrence; "they'll never dare do such a thing as that!"

"They'll dare fast enough," said Leroy; "but they shall never do it! They'll try me first!"

A sudden light broke over me. Leroy's hesitation and dubious statements might have this meaning. He might himself suspect Janet of the crime, and he might be determined to be let himself thought guilty in her place. This didn't quite explain the key, but I hadn't thought it out thoroughly yet, and if for quixotic reasons he wanted to make it appear that he was implicated, he had certainly made a good start. Alas, every new development pointed or might be construed to point toward Janet. I longed for a frank talk with Leroy, but I knew that would be impracticable. For if he intended to muddle the case and direct suspicion toward himself in order to turn it away from Janet, he would pursue those same tactics with me. And beside, although he hid it, I well knew that he was chagrined and angry at the fact of my being chosen for Janet's lawyer instead of himself. So I discarded any hope I might have formed of getting the truth out of Leroy, and left that to the official authorities.

At present, Leroy's intention seemed to be to discard all question of crime or criminal, and attend to the business in hand of Mr. Pembroke's will.

I myself saw no necessity for immediate proceedings in this matter, but Leroy insisted upon it, and insisted too, that both Janet and George should go with him at once into the Pembroke

110

apartment, where, he said, there were papers and documents necessary at the moment.

The fact that I was not invited to accompany them, was made so patent that I had no desire to intrude my presence, although as Miss Pembroke's lawyer I could have done so. But I concluded that one reason for Leroy's haste to get at those papers, was his wish to get rid of me. Nor was it entirely to be wondered at that he should want an interview alone with the two cousins. I was a comparative stranger to him, my sister an entire stranger; whereas he had been for years a friend of the Pembroke household. And so the three went away to the apartment across the hall; and I was left alone with Laura.

The door had scarcely closed behind them, before Laura spoke her mind. "That Leroy is the guilty man," she said; "don't say, 'how did he get in?' for I don't know, and I don't care! But he's the one who killed Mr. Pembroke, and he had his own motive for doing so, which we know nothing about."

"While all that may be true, Laura," I said, in a conciliatory way, for she was very much excited, "yet you must not make such positive statements, with so little to base them on. Leroy may have a guilty knowledge of the matter, but I don't believe he murdered Mr. Pembroke, and I do believe he's letting himself be suspected to shield Janet."

"Nothing of the sort," declared Laura; "he's a bad man! I don't have to see him twice to know that. And if he isn't guilty, and if he's letting himself be suspected,—then it's to implicate Janet and not to save her!"

"Laura, you're crazy. How could his implication also implicate her?"

"Why, don't you see? if they think Mr. Leroy committed the crime, they'll try to find out how he got in. And then they'll conclude that Janet let him in. Because you know, Otis, there was really no other way anybody could get in. And then, you see, they'll conclude that Mr. Leroy and Janet acted together, and are both guilty."

"Laura, you argue just like a woman; you say anything that comes into your head, and then back it up with some other absurd idea! Now, sister, talk to me in this strain all you want to, but let me beg of you never to say these things to anyone else."

Laura looked a little offended, but she was too fond of me ever really to resent anything I said to her, so she smiled, and forgave my aspersions on her reasoning powers.

But I couldn't help remembering that Janet had told me that Leroy was untrustworthy, and not entirely reliable, and now that Laura, with her woman's intuition, had denounced him, I began to wonder myself what sort of a man Leroy really was.

XVIII

THE ROOMS IN WASHINGTON SQUARE

In sheer desperation, I resolved upon an interview with Inspector Crawford. I hadn't a very high opinion of him as a detective, but I had reached the pitch where I must do something.

I telephoned to him, but it was only after some persistence that I could persuade him to give me even a little of his valuable time. Finally he agreed to a fifteen-minute interview at his own home.

It was not far to his house, and as I walked over there I wondered why he seemed so averse to a discussion of the Pembroke case. He had impressed me, when I saw him that morning, as one of those busybodies in the detective line who are always willing to dilate upon their clues and their deductions, their theories and their inferences.

But as soon as I began to talk with Mr. Crawford I learned that he had little interest in the Pembroke case, because he considered its result a foregone conclusion.

Inspector Crawford was not an especially cultured man, nor of a particularly affable nature, but he was possessed, as I soon learned, of a certain stubbornness which manifested itself mainly in adhering firmly to his own decisions.

"I know Miss Pembroke killed her uncle," he said, "because nobody else could by any possibility have done it. I examined the windows myself. Those which were fastened were absolutely immovable from the outside, and those which were unfastened had the same sort of catches, and the black woman declared she had unfastened them from the inside in the morning. The window opening on the fire escape had a double lock, the dumb-waiter was securely bolted on the kitchen side, the night-latch and chain were on the front door, and, therefore, my dear sir, to get into that apartment without breaking something was as impossible as if it had been hermetically sealed."

"Some one might have cut out a pane of glass and replaced it," I suggested.

The inspector looked at me with a glance almost of pity.

"It's my business to make sure of such things," he said. "Of course I thought of that, and examined every window-pane. Had one been put in with fresh putty during the night, I should certainly have detected it. If you examine them, you will find both putty and paint hard and weather-stained."

My respect for Mr. Crawford's detective ability rose rapidly, and I frankly told him so.

He smiled disinterestedly.

"I'm not one of those spectacular detectives," he said, "who pick up a handkerchief in the street, and declare at once that it was dropped by a cross-eyed lady with one front tooth missing, who was on her way to visit her step-daughter now living in Jamaica, Long Island, but who formerly was a governess in a doctor's family in Meriden, Connecticut."

I laughed at this bit of sarcasm, but was too vitally interested in the subject in hand to care for amusing side issues.

"Do you say then, inspector," I continued, "that there was positively no way for any one else to get into that apartment, and that therefore Mr. Pembroke necessarily met his death at the hands of his niece or the colored servant?"

"Or both," added Mr. Crawford.

"You assert that as your unqualified opinion?"

"I assert it as an incontrovertible fact," said Inspector Crawford, in his decided way, "and, though it needs no backing up of evidence, the evidence all points unmistakably to the same fact. There are motive, opportunity, and a weapon at hand. What more is there to say?"

"There is only this to say," I declared, maddened by his air of finality: "that Miss Pembroke did not do it; that neither she nor the black woman knows who did do it; and that I take it upon myself to prove this when the occasion shall arise to do so."

Again the inspector looked at me with that compassionate expression that irritated me beyond words.

"Mr. Landon," he said, "I have no desire to be personal, but may I ask you, if you were as absolutely disinterested in the Pembroke case as I am, would you not incline to my opinion?"

This silenced me, for I well knew that but for my interest in Janet Pembroke I should inevitably be forced to Mr. Crawford's point of view.

"Ah!" he said. "I thought so. Now let me tell you, Mr. Landon— and I am indeed sorry to tell you—that there is no possible way to get that girl acquitted, and that your best plan is to work simply for the lightest possible penalty. If you can plead self-defence, temporary insanity, or even somnambulism, I advise you to do so."

"I thank you, inspector, for your advice, and regret to say that I cannot follow it. I shall plead 'not guilty,' and I shall prove my case."

The inspector began to look interested, for, though a man may not boast of his own reputation, I may say that Mr. Crawford knew me as a lawyer of long practice and wide experience; and knew, too, that I had been successful in cases where wise and anxious judges had scarcely dared hope for it.

"I hope it may be so," he said. "It does not seem to be possible, but, of course, no man's judgment is infallible. Might I be allowed, however, to ask your line of defence?"

"I don't know exactly, myself," I confessed; "but I think it will implicate George Lawrence."

"But he couldn't get in."

"Inspector, if any one is implicated other than those two women, it must necessarily be some one who 'couldn't get in.'"

"That is true," said the inspector; "but, all the same, a murder can't be committed by a man who can't get in."

"That is no more impossible," I said stanchly, "than a murder committed by either of those two women."

Again the inspector contented himself with a smile.

"I have no reason," I went on, "for suspecting George Lawrence, except that he could be said to have a motive. I admit, as you say, that it does not seem possible for him to have entered the apartment, unless one of the women let him in."

"Let him in!" echoed the inspector. "I hadn't thought of that! Ah, now I see your idea. If George Lawrence is the man who did the deed and was let in by his cousin, while she might have been accessory, she might not have known of the deed at all."

"That is possible, inspector," I agreed; "but had she let George in, she must again have put the chain on the door after he went out. This is scarcely compatible with the assumption that she knew nothing of what had happened in the meantime."

"No," declared the inspector, in his decided way. "Your suggestion, however, leads to a new line of investigation. But say George Lawrence had gone to the Pembrokes' apartment last night, and had come away again, the elevator boy would have known it, and would have given evidence this morning; that is, unless he had been bribed, which is, of course, possible. But all this will be brought out at the trial."

"Not so fast, inspector," I said, feeling a grim delight in bringing him up with a round turn. "George Lawrence can prove a complete and perfect alibi, attested by responsible witnesses."

Inspector Crawford looked thoroughly disgusted. "Then the whole matter stands where it did at first," he said, "though, of course, we must remember that, since the women could have let in George Lawrence, they could, of course, have let in any one else, had they been so minded. But all this is in your province, rather than in mine, and if you can find anybody who is likely to have gone in there last night, with or without criminal intent, I think for your own sake you had better make investigation along that line."

"Mr. Crawford," I said, "I would not have mentioned to you even the name of George Lawrence in this connection if I could have done what I wanted to without your assistance. I want to go to George Lawrence's apartment, and make a search of his rooms. I have not a definite reason for doing this, but I feel that it may lead to something. I cannot say I suspect George Lawrence of the crime. I cannot doubt his alibi, nor can I imagine how he could have gotten into the apartment had he wanted to. But I do know that he had, or at least might possibly have had, a motive for desiring his uncle's death, and upon that perhaps irrelevant fact I base what I shall not call a suspicion, but an interest into looking into his affairs. I could not go through his rooms alone, but as an inspector you will be allowed to do so, and I want to go with you and at once."

I may have been mistaken in Mr. Crawford's inclination toward detective work. Although he had seemed indifferent when he had been so sure of his conclusion, the mere opportunity of searching for clues seemed to stir him to action, and, to my surprise, he was not only willing but anxious to go with me at once.

As I knew Lawrence would spend the entire afternoon in his work of looking over Mr. Pembroke's papers, I felt that the coast was clear for an hour or so, at least. So together we took a Broadway car, and were not long in reaching Washington Square.

The inspector's badge, of course, gained him access at once to George's apartment, and I followed him into the rooms, feeling that if there was anything even remotely approaching a clue, I must and would find it.

Though not luxurious, Lawrence's quarters were exceedingly comfortable. There was a studio, not large, but well lighted and furnished in a way that showed its use as a living-room, and perhaps for small social functions as well. A bedroom and bath completed the suite, and the inspector told me to begin my search.

"Let us examine the place," he said, "independently of each other, and afterward we can compare notes. I confess I have little hope of finding evidence of any sort. Of course I don't for a moment think that, even had Lawrence killed his uncle, he would have broken off that hat-pin and brought it home here to incriminate himself."

"Of course not," I assented; "but, by the way, where is the other half of that hat-pin?"

The inspector gave his queer smile. "Assuming a woman to have done the deed," he said, "we must assume her to be clever enough to dispose of a piece of a broken hat-pin."

My heart sank at his words, for I saw how deeply rooted was his belief in Janet's guilt, and I feared a judge and jury might look at it in the same way.

Silently we began our search. I took the studio, and the inspector the bedroom, first; afterward we were to go over each other's ground.

In one way, it seemed a dreadful thing to be poking round among a man's personal belongings; but again, since the cause of justice demanded it, I felt no hesitancy in doing so.

I took little interest in the sketches on the walls or the odd bits of junk and curios on the tables. No man with anything to conceal would leave it in those obvious places.

And yet I was not looking for anything George might have concealed, but rather for some straw which might show the direction of the wind of evidence.

For the first time in my life, I felt like the detective in fiction, and I scrutinized carefully the floor and the rug. It seemed to me that all the clues I had ever read of had been discovered on the floor; but the trouble was that this floor offered so many unexpected substances that the result was distracting. But by no stretch of the imagination could I look upon them as clues. I certainly discovered many things upon the floor that told their own story; but the stories were of no importance. Cigarette or cigar ashes were in such quantity as to indicate recent masculine guests. An artificial violet and a bit of fluffy feather trimming showed perhaps an afternoon tea, or a reception which feminine guests had attended. Lead-pencil shavings here and there betokened the untidiness of an artist, and splashes of ink or water-color, though numerous, proved merely that Lawrence had spoken the truth regarding his profession.

Though disheartened by my non-success, I kept on until I had examined every square inch of floor. I found nothing unexplainable to the most ordinary intellect, except a few tiny bits of broken glass on the hearthstone. So infinitesimal were these fragments that I almost missed them, and, though I could not think them of any importance, I took them up on a bit of white paper and examined them by the light. They were of a pinkish purple color, and I wondered if they could be bits of a druggist's phial which had contained poison. The notion was absurd enough, for Mr. Pembroke had not been poisoned, and, moreover, even granting my hypothesis a true one, those few specks of glass would represent only a small fraction of a broken bottle.

But he might have dropped it, my imagination rambled on, and smashed it, and then swept up all the fragments, as he thought, but overlooked these specks.

116

At any rate, I put the paper containing the bits in my pocket, and went on with my search. Feeling that I had finished the floor, I examined all the furniture and decorations, paying no attention to Lawrence's desk or personal belongings.

Mr. Crawford came in from the bedroom. "I've done up my room," he said, "and there's nothing there at all, not even a revolver. Now, if you're through here, we will change territory."

"I can't find anything," I returned, and as I spoke the inspector went straight to the writing-desk.

"If there is nothing here," he said, "I give it up."

With a practised hand he ran swiftly through Lawrence's papers.

"H'm!" he said. "Our young friend has been dabbling in stocks. Bought L. & C. Q. on a margin. That's bad, for it dropped 'way down day before yesterday. That ought to help along your 'motive,' Mr. Landon, for as sure as I sit here George Lawrence must have lost many thousands in Wall Street on Wednesday."

"It is corroborative," I said, "but that's all. Granting Lawrence's motive for desiring to inherit his uncle's money at once, there is no real evidence that he helped matters along by putting the old gentleman out of the way."

"Not a bit," agreed Inspector Crawford; "and you mark my word, Mr. Landon, if there was any reason for suspecting young Lawrence, it would have turned up before this."

"I'm not so sure of that," I returned; "and it isn't exactly evidence I'm after, but merely a hint as to how he could have done it."

"Ah!" said the inspector, smiling again. "He couldn't have done it save with the knowledge and assistance of his cousin."

XIX

A TALK WITH JANET

I went home decidedly disheartened. As usual, the Inspector's positiveness and incontrovertible reasoning depressed my spirits, because I felt convinced, although against my will, that he might be right.

But when I entered our apartment, and found Laura and Janet waiting for me, I forgot my troubles in the happiness of seeing Janet in my home.

The girl must have been of an adaptable temperament, for surely our household was totally unlike the one she had been accustomed to, and yet she seemed perfectly at home and at ease with us.

She wore black, but her robes of soft trailing silk, with a sort of transparent net by way of a yoke, did not seem so unsightly as heavy crape-trimmed dresses had always appeared to me.

Indeed the soft dull black was very becoming to Janet, and threw out her creamy white skin in beautiful relief. Her large dark eyes and dusky hair completed the harmony of black and white, and her scarlet lips were the only touch of color in the picture.

The evening was a trifle chill, and Laura had a wood fire blazing in the grate, for even in the short time we had lived in the Hammersleigh, my energetic sister had succeeded in substituting open fires for the ornate but unsatisfactory gas logs.

And so it was a cosy picture of home life that met my eyes, as I entered after my expedition down to Washington Square.

Of course, I couldn't mention my afternoon's experiences just then, for it was almost dinner time and I knew Laura's aversion to unpleasant subjects of conversation at the dinner table.

And so I did my part toward making the meal a cheery and pleasant occasion; and it was less difficult than might have been expected to avoid all reference to the tragedy.

Both women were quite willing to follow my lead, and our talk was of all sorts of pleasant matters, and now and then even verged toward lightness. I realized, as I was sure Laura did too, that Janet was a delightful conversationalist. She was both receptive and responsive. She caught a point easily and was quick at repartee. Moreover, she was gentle and refined, and it is needless to say that my love for her grew apace with my discovery of her merits.

After dinner we returned to the drawing-room, and with her

usual tact, Laura contrived a household errand of some nature that took her away for a time, and left me alone with my client.

I was all unwilling to break the charm of the pleasant atmosphere we had created, but I knew it must be done if I were to free Janet from suspicion.

Determined to learn from her some facts which would help me, I told her at once that I desired a straightforward talk with her.

Immediately her manner changed. She became once more reserved, haughty and rebellious. But I had no choice save to go on.

"I am so sorry," I said, "that you resent my questioning you about these things. For surely, Miss Pembroke, you must understand, and it is my duty to make you understand that your position is serious. Now whether you want to or not, won't you please be honest with me, and confide more fully in me what knowledge you may have bearing on the case?"

"I can't be honest," she replied, with a sigh that seemed to come from her very soul; "I truly can't. Whatever you learn must be without my assistance."

"Why can you not be honest? Are you afraid to be?"

"I cannot answer that question, either. I tell you, Mr. Landon, that I have no information of any sort to give you."

"Then I must ask you a few definite questions, and you must answer them. Why did you not mention the letter that came to your uncle from Jonathan Scudder?"

"Who told you about that?"

The girl started up as if I had accused her of something serious, and indeed perhaps it was.

"The Inspector found the letter in your room," I replied; "as you were not willing to be frank in these matters, the law took its rights and searched the whole place for any possible light on the subject."

"And you consider that that letter throws light on the subject?"

"Only to the extent of proving that you purposely suppressed that letter; and I ask you why?"

"And I refuse to tell you why."

"Miss Pembroke, don't do that. Truly, you injure your own cause by refusing to tell these things. You have taken me for your lawyer; now if you want me to help you, indeed I may almost say to rescue you, from the danger you are in, you must help me in any way that you can."

My earnestness seemed to have an effect. The girl's face softened and her voice trembled a little as she said, "Perhaps it would be better for me to tell you all,—but,—no, I can't, I can't!" She hid her face in her hands, and her whole slender form shook with emotion. But she did not cry, as I had feared she would. Instead, she

119

raised her head with a sudden determined gesture. "There was no reason," she said, with an air of indifference which I knew was assumed; "I simply forgot it, that's all."

"You forgot it!" I said, looking her straight in the eyes, so earnestly, that her own eyes fell before mine.

I knew she could not persist in a falsehood long, and sure enough in a moment she said, "Well, at least I didn't exactly forget it, but I thought it was of no consequence."

"You thought it was of no consequence! when only last evening we were discussing J. S. with your cousin, and wondering who he could be. At that time you had read the letter from Jonathan Scudder, saying that he would not come here Wednesday evening as he had telegraphed that he would do. Why did you not tell us of it?"

"Perhaps it wasn't the same J. S.!" Janet smiled at me as she said this, and I felt sure the smile was to distract me from my serious purpose, and win me to a lighter mood. And she nearly succeeded, too, for again I saw gentleness in her smile, and when to Janet Pembroke's beautiful face was added the charm of gentleness, it was irresistible indeed.

But by a mighty effort I refrained from being cajoled, and I said sternly, "You knew it was the same J. S., because the letter referred to the telegram."

"That's so," she said, musingly; "I never thought of that. I fear I'm not very clever at deception."

"I fear you are not," I answered, gravely, "and I thank Heaven for it. Now, if you will just put all these matters into my hands, and tell me what I ask, you will have no further cause for deception, and, I hope, no more trouble."

"What do you ask?" she said, and never before had she looked so lovely. She spoke in a low tone and had she been the most finished coquette she could not have appeared more alluring. I was tempted almost beyond my strength to clasp her in my arms and say, "I ask only for you," but I knew were I to precipitate matters in that way I might antagonize her, and so lose what slight chance I had of helping her.

"I ask," I said, in low even tones, "that you will tell me frankly why you made no mention of the letter from Jonathan Scudder?"

"Because I wished suspicion to rest upon J. S.!" The words were quick and incisive, and fairly cut into the air as she enunciated them clearly and emphatically.

"Do you know Jonathan Scudder?"

"I do not. I never heard the name until I read that letter. But I know J. S. to be an enemy of my uncle, and why may it not be that

120

he came and killed Uncle Robert, even after he sent that letter? Perhaps he sent it for a blind."

"Miss Pembroke, you do not believe J. S. came at all on Wednesday night. You know he did not, and you are making this up simply that suspicion may be turned in his direction. Is not this true?"

"Yes," faintly murmured the girl, "you asked me to be frank, and I have been."

She was making an awful admission, and she was perfectly well aware of it. Fear clutched at my heart. If she herself had killed her uncle, how natural to endeavor to throw suspicion on an unknown man. Again, if Leroy were implicated, or if they had been companions in wrong-doing how equally plausible a ruse!

Her face was white now to the very lips. Her hands trembled, and her eyes darted frightened glances, as if she knew not which way to turn next.

"Miss Pembroke," I said, very gently, "I'm more sorry than I can tell you, that you persist in secrecy. But since you do I will speak for you. You want to throw suspicion on J. S., in order to divert it either from yourself or from someone else whom you wish to shield."

"How do you know that?" cried Janet, looking up with startled eyes.

"It is not difficult to guess," I said, bitterly. "Nor is it difficult to guess the identity of the one you might wish to shield."

"Don't!" breathed Janet, clasping her hands; "don't breathe his name aloud!"

"I will!" I said, thoroughly angered now; "it is Graham Leroy, and you do love him, in spite of your pretended dislike of him!"

I paused suddenly, for a new thought had struck me. If Leroy were the murderer, and if Janet had admitted him to the house, and willingly or unwillingly been cognizant of his deed, then she would act exactly the way she had acted! She would try to shield him, try to avert suspicion from him, but of course she could not have him for her lawyer, and though she still loved him, she could not but scorn him.

The suddenness of these thoughts so overwhelmed me that for a moment I did not look at her. When I did, I was amazed at the change in her face. From a white pallor it had turned to an angry red, and my heart fell as I realized that she was angry at me for discovering her secret.

"Don't look like that," I pleaded; "only tell me the truth, and I will help you,—I will help you both. At any rate, I know that you were guiltless, even if you have a guilty knowledge of Leroy's deed."

"You needn't assume me guiltless," Janet said, and her low

121

voice destitute of inflection, sounded as if she were forcing herself to recite, parrot-like, a lesson already learned. "I had motive, and Mr. Leroy had none."

"He may have had a dozen motives, for all I know," I said, rather harshly, for I was beginning to realize that if she cared enough for Leroy to proclaim herself guilty, my hopes were small indeed. "He may have wanted that money himself, and come back to get it!" This was a mean speech on my part, and utterly unfounded, but I was so angry at Janet for shielding Leroy's name, that I cared little what I said.

"Oh, Mr. Leroy never wanted money; he's a very rich man."

"Who did want the money then? Did you?" I was fast forgetting my manners, and my determination to win Janet's confidence by kindliness, but I had not expected to have Leroy thus flung in my face.

"Yes, I wanted money," said Janet, "you learned that from Charlotte's evidence."

"You are the strangest girl!" I said, staring at her, "you won't tell me the simple things I ask, and then you fire a statement like that at me! What do you mean? That you really wanted a large sum of money?"

"Yes; ten thousand dollars." The girl whispered this, and it seemed to my bewildered fancy as if she said it without even her own volition. It seemed forced from her by some subconscious process, and I was both amazed and frightened. But I tried not to show my feelings, for if I would learn the truth of this surprising revelation, I must move carefully.

"Did you want that much?" I said, in a casual way, as if it were a mere nominal sum. "What did you want it for?"

"As if I should tell you that!" and this astounding piece of humanity tossed her head, and smiled almost roguishly at me.

"Never mind what you wanted it for," I said, "but you did want it, didn't you? And you asked your uncle for it, and he refused you."

"He said that if,—if I would,—would—oh, what am I saying!" She broke off with a little gasp, as if she had almost betrayed a secret. But I knew.

"He said he would give it to you, and more too, if you would marry Mr. Leroy, didn't he?"

"Yes," Janet replied, and this time she spoke in a simple, natural voice and looked at me frankly.

"But, as you wanted the money to give to Mr. Leroy, and didn't want to marry him, your uncle's proposition didn't please you?"

Janet looked at me in a bewildered way. "Yes," she stammered, "yes,—that was it."

But I was learning my girl at last. For some reason she was telling a string of falsehoods! My faith in her made me believe that she was doing this for some definite and, to her, justifiable purpose. And yet, though my suggestion about Leroy seemed to me to be in line with her plans, and though she had said yes to it,—yet I knew it was not the truth. My rapidly increasing love for her gave me an insight into her nature, and though I might not be able to persuade her to tell me the truth, yet I could discern when she spoke truly and when falsely.

"I give it up," I said to her, suddenly adopting a lighter tone; "I can do nothing with you tonight in our relations of client and lawyer. Let us drop the whole dreadful subject for the rest of this evening, and let us pretend that we are just good friends, with no troublesome questions between us.

"Yes," agreed Janet, with a smile of delight, "let us do that; but anyway, I don't see why the troublesome questions that come between us as lawyer and client, should interfere with our friendship."

"Nor do I, bless you!" I exclaimed, and with a lightened heart I put aside my burden of doubt and fear for the present. And soon Laura came back, and we all chatted pleasantly, without reference to anything gruesome or dreadful.

Laura had not heard our foregoing conversation, and had not, as I feared I had, additional reasons to wonder at Janet Pembroke.

But, we were both charmed with the girl's vivacity and entertaining powers. She did or said nothing which savored too much of gayety to harmonize with her black gown, and yet her little whimsical speeches and her gentle wistful smiles won our hearts anew, and made both Laura and myself feel bound to her without regard to the cloud that hung above her head.

123

XX

THE INITIALED HANDKERCHIEF

The funeral of Robert Pembroke was to be held Saturday afternoon. The man had so few friends that elaborate services were not arranged for. Indeed it was to take place from the mortuary chapel, and would doubtless be attended by a very small assembly.

Of course Laura and I would go, out of respect for our friends, although we had never known Mr. Pembroke himself.

I did not see Janet before I went downtown Saturday morning, as Laura was taking great care of the girl, and never allowed her to appear early in the morning.

When I reached my office, I found a letter which was signed James Decker.

It was a bit illiterate, but it revealed to me the fact that its writer had attended the National Theatre on the night of October sixteenth and as he had occupied a seat H 3, he was behind G 3, he wanted very much to know in what way it was to his advantage to announce the fact to me.

I telephoned Mr. Decker at the address he gave, and he agreed to come to see me within the next hour.

He came very soon, and entirely fulfilled the mental picture I had already drawn of him. Flashy clothing, red necktie and hat on the back of his head were his distinguishing characteristics, with voice and manner to correspond.

"What's up, pard?" was his unduly familiar greeting, but though I did not respond in his vernacular, I had no wish to criticise it.

I explained to him that I wanted to know anything he could tell me about the occupants of seats one and three G on the night in question.

"Sure, I can tell ye all about 'em," he declared; "they was pals of mine, Billy Rivers and Bob Pierson. They was eight of us went, and we had aisle seats of four rows, right in front of each other. What about them two chaps? they're all right, Guv'nor, I'll go bail for that!"

"I've no doubt of it, Mr. Decker," I responded, heartily; "and as this is just a little private matter between you and me, I'm going to ask you for their addresses, but I am going to assure you that this will get them into no trouble, unless they deserve it; and that if you so desire, your name need not be mentioned in the matter."

"Great Mackerel! I don't care how much you mention my name,

and like's not Bob and Bill won't care either. They're straight, mister, good pals and good men."

There was something about the candid gaze of Decker that made me feel confidence in his words. I had a conviction then and there, that whoever murdered Robert Pembroke it was neither Bob nor Bill, the good friends of James Decker. But in a way, it was a disappointment, for it only proved one more clue worthless. Where those two ticket stubs came from, or how they got into Robert Pembroke's bedroom, I didn't then stop to think; although I had hazy ideas of tracing some sort of connection with the elevator boy or janitor and these people. But for the moment, all I could do was to take these men's addresses, and present Mr. Decker with a sufficient honorarium to pay him for the trouble and exertion of coming to see me.

I went home at noon, pondering over those ticket stubs. After all, perhaps I had been terribly taken in. Perhaps this Decker man made up the whole story for the purpose of getting the fee which he knew I was pretty sure to give him. Perhaps his two pals were as imaginary as they were good, and perhaps he was only a clever adventurer who had succeeded in fooling a less clever lawyer! Well at any rate, I had done no harm, and I had the men's addresses. Later on, I would tell the District Attorney the whole story, and if he chose to follow it up he could do so.

From the funeral of Robert Pembroke I went straight to the District Attorney's office.

I had come to the conclusion that I must do something, and that I must do it quickly. I knew Buckner was only waiting till the funeral was over to push his investigations; and I knew too, that unless some new evidence was forthcoming from somewhere, his procedure must inevitably result in the arrest of Janet.

I must find that new evidence, which must at least turn the trend of suspicion in some other direction. I could think only of the handkerchief that I had found in Mr. Pembroke's bedroom. This had never been accounted for in any way, and surely it must mean something.

The other articles I had found had proved of little value so far. The ticket stubs promised little or nothing, for I could not feel that the man Decker or his friends were implicated. The time-table gave me no idea of where to look for any clue. It was useless to refer it to the Lackawanna Railroad. Moreover, East Lynnwood was not on that road, nor was Utica, and these were the only two places that had so much as been mentioned in connection with the affair.

The torn telegram, in connection with the letter, seemed to

mean nothing; or if it did, it pointed toward Janet's deception in regard to it.

The money was gone, and that, too, in the minds of some people, again suggested Janet's wrong-doing. The key, while it might seem to implicate Leroy, was far from being a definite clue, and if it meant Leroy, it might also mean Janet's complicity.

The hair-pin I left out of consideration, and as a last resort, I determined to run down the owner of that handkerchief.

I rehearsed all these conclusions to the District Attorney, and he smiled a little superciliously. It is strange how the police officials scorn the interesting clues so beloved of the detective mind.

However, Buckner said nothing in opposition to my plan, and at my request handed me the handkerchief. We had little conversation but it was plain to be seen that he was assured of Janet's guilt and saw no other direction in which to look for the criminal.

"Go ahead and investigate that handkerchief business," he said, "but you'll find it leads to nothing. That handkerchief might have been left there by any caller during the last week or so; and as we know Mr. Pembroke had frequent callers, that is of course the explanation."

I couldn't believe this, because, though now crumpled from passing through many hands, when I had found the handkerchief it was comparatively fresh, and looked as if it had but just been shaken from its laundered folds. This would seem to indicate that it had not been in the room long, and moreover had it been left there several days before, it would have been found by Charlotte or by Janet, and laid aside to be restored to its owner.

I put it in my pocket, and after a short further conversation with Mr. Buckner, I was convinced afresh of Janet's impending danger, so that I went away spurred to my utmost endeavor to find some new information.

I examined the handkerchief carefully, but saw only what I had already observed; that it was unusually fine and dainty for a man's possession, and that the embroidered letters were of exquisite workmanship and unique design.

I took a taxicab and began a systematic canvass of the best shops in the city that provided wearing apparel for fastidious men.

The results were not encouraging. One after another, the haberdashers informed me that the handkerchief had not come from their shops. Indeed, they opined that the work had not been done in this country, but that the handkerchief had been bought abroad. However, as I was about to give up my search, one interested shopkeeper told me of a small and very exclusive establishment from which that handkerchief might have been obtained.

With my hopes a trifle buoyed up, I went at once to the address given me, and to my delight the affable cleric recognized the handkerchief.

"Yes," he said, "that is one of ours. We have them hand-embroidered for one of our best customers. He has used that design for many years. Did he recommend you to come here?"

"No," said I, "I'm not ordering handkerchiefs for myself. Moreover, I was not sent here by the owner of this one, nor do I know his name. Are you willing to tell it to me?"

"I see no reason why I shouldn't. That handkerchief belongs to Mr. Gresham,—William Sydney Gresham. It is one of the best bits of work we ever put out, and we are a little proud of it."

"It's beautiful work," I agreed, "and now will you give me Mr. Gresham's address?"

Although not especially keen-witted, the clerk looked a little surprised at this, and hesitated for a moment. But when I told him that the matter was important, he made no further objection, and gave me Mr. Gresham's club address.

Needless to say I went directly there, and by good luck I found Mr. Gresham, pleasantly passing the before dinner hour with some of his friends.

I went to him, introduced myself and asked for a moment's private conversation. He looked surprised, but consented, and with a courteous manner led me to a small room, where we were alone.

"Be seated, Mr. Landon," he said, pleasantly; "what can I do for you?"

He was a handsome man and well set up. He was especially well dressed, in clothes of English cut, and his whole appearance showed attention to details. His face betokened a strong, manly character and his gaze was clear and straightforward.

Without preliminaries, I showed him the handkerchief and said, simply, "Is this your handkerchief, Mr. Gresham?"

"It certainly is," he said, taking the linen square, and glancing at the letters; "did you find it? I thank you very much for restoring my property,—though of no great value."

"Had you missed it?" I said, looking at him closely.

"Bless my soul, no! A man has several handkerchiefs, you know, and I dare say I might lose two or three without missing them. Excuse me, Mr. Landon, but aren't you attaching undue importance to such a trifle as a lost handkerchief?"

"I don't know yet, Mr. Gresham, whether this particular loss of

127

yours will prove to be a trifling matter or not. Do you know Robert Pembroke?"

"The man who was murdered a few days ago?"

"Yes."

"No, I never knew him; but I read in the papers of the poor fellow's death and thought it most shocking. I trust they will discover the murderer and avenge the crime."

If Mr. Gresham were implicated in the affair, he certainly carried off this conversation with a fine composure. But I resolved to startle his calm if I could.

"Then can you explain, Mr. Gresham," I said, "how this handkerchief of yours happened to be found on the bed of the murdered man the morning after the murder?"

"Great Heavens, no! nor do I believe it was found there!"

"But it was, for I myself found it."

"My handkerchief! In Mr. Pembroke's bedroom! Impossible!"

The man spoke with an angry inflection and a rising color, and I watched him narrowly. Either this was the just indignation of an innocent man, or else it was the carefully rehearsed dissimulation of a clever wrong-doer. My instinct and my reason told me he was innocent, but my inclinations so strongly hoped for some hint of his guilt, that I persevered.

"Yes, Mr. Gresham, I found it in that room, and on that bed in less than twelve hours after Mr. Pembroke was killed."

"You did! and you think therefore that I killed him, or at least that I was in his room! Why, man, I have already told you that I never knew Mr. Pembroke, and have certainly never been to his house, nor do I even know where he lives!"

This was all very well if it were true, but how was I to know whether this fine gentleman were lying or not. To be sure his face, voice and manner gave every effect of outraged innocence, but was that not just what a clever criminal would show?

"Where were you late last Wednesday night?" I asked him bluntly.

"By Jove! I don't know! I may have been in a dozen places. I go where I choose, and I don't keep a diary of my doings!"

"But try to think, Mr. Gresham," I said, more gently; "were you here at this club?"

"I may have been and I may not. I may have been motoring, or dining out, or at the theatre, or anywhere. I tell you I don't know where I was."

"It will be to your own interest to remember," I said, speaking sternly, for now I began to suspect the man.

"Why do you say that?"

128

"Because when a man's handkerchief is found under such circumstances, it is advisable for the man to prove that he was not there too."

"Lest I be suspected of the murder of a man whom I never saw, and never even heard of until after he was dead?"

"We have only your own word for that," I returned, coldly; "but the rather definite clue of your handkerchief found in Mr. Pembroke's bedroom requires investigation, and I am here for that purpose."

"The deuce you are! Well, Mr. Landon, you are barking up the wrong tree! May I refer you to my man of business, and ask you to excuse me from a further discussion of this matter?"

"You may not! I am here, Mr. Gresham, if not exactly in an official capacity, yet with the authority of a lawyer employed on this case. And if I may advise you, merely as man to man, I think it will be better for you to question your memory a little more closely, and endeavor to recollect where you were on Wednesday night."

"Oh, suppose I can hark back to it. Let me see; I believe I motored up to Greenwich for the night. No, that was Tuesday night. And Thursday night I went to the theatre. Well, then it must have been Wednesday night that I was at the Hardings' to dinner. Yes, I was. I dined at the home of James S. Harding. And that you can verify from him. Now are you satisfied?"

"What time did you leave Mr. Harding's?"

"I don't know; about eleven or twelve, I suppose."

"And then where did you go?"

"Good Heavens! I can't remember every corner I turned! I think I stopped here at the Club before I went to my diggings; yes I'm sure I did."

"Then there must be Club members, or even stewards by whom you can prove an alibi."

"Prove an alibi! Look here, Mr. Landon, I positively refuse to carry this conversation further. I know nothing of your Mr. Pembroke or of his murderer. I know nothing about that handkerchief, which you say you found there, except the fact that it is mine. Now if your people want to arrest me, let them come and do it; but until they do, kindly spare me further questioning, which I do not admit to be within your rights. Allow me to wish you good morning."

Though most anxious to believe this man guilty, it was difficult to do so, and yet I was quite willing to believe that his somewhat grandiloquent attitude was all a bluff. However, I had found the owner of the handkerchief, and I had learned all I could from him. And so, with a conventional leave-taking, I left him and went home.

129

XXI

FLEMING STONE

At dinner and during Saturday evening, Janet seemed so sad and depressed in spirits, that I seconded Laura's efforts to divert her mind from all thoughts of the tragedy.

It was not so difficult as it might seem, for the girl's strange temperament was volatile, and her thoughts were easily led to any subject we suggested. We talked of books and music, and finally of personal acquaintances, discovering that we had a few in common. Although I did not know the Warings personally they were acquaintances of some friends of mine, and I gathered from Janet's remarks that Millicent Waring was one of her intimates.

The evening passed pleasantly enough, but after Laura had carried Janet away to rest for the night, I sat and pondered deeply over my case.

Try as I would, I could not feel that Mr. Gresham had any guilty knowledge of the affair; and if he had, I could think of no way to turn suspicion in his direction. Except, of course, through the handkerchief, which now seemed to me an insoluble mystery.

And except for the slender hope resting upon that handkerchief, I had nothing to offer in the way of evidence against any person or persons other than the girl I loved. It was then that I bethought me of Fleming Stone. I had recently heard of the marvellous work this great detective had done in the Maxwell case, and I wondered that I had not thought of him before. Beside his powers the efforts of minor detectives paled into insignificance. His services were expensive, I knew, but George Lawrence had authorized the employment of a detective, and I did not believe he would object to the outlay. Then, too, my client was now a rich woman, or would be, as soon as the estate was settled.

I admitted my own inability to read the mystery in the clues I had at my disposal, but I felt sure that Stone could do so.

Then the horrible thought struck me, what if Stone's inexorable finger should point toward Janet! But this I would not allow myself to consider, for I could not believe it possible; and, moreover, without Stone's intervention, the law was determined to accuse Janet, anyway, therefore Stone's help was the only possible chance I could see for help.

And so I went to bed with a hopeful heart, that since truth must triumph, and since Fleming Stone could discover the truth if any one could, that Janet's exoneration was practically assured.

I was uncertain whether or not to tell Janet of my decision to consult Fleming Stone. And all Sunday morning I hesitated about the matter.

It was late Sunday afternoon before I concluded that it would be better to inform her of my plan, and this conclusion was really brought about more by opportunity than by decision.

Laura had gone out, and Janet and I sat alone in our pleasant library. The girl looked so sweet and dear, in her pathetic black robes, that my heart yearned to comfort her. Her face was sad and very gentle of expression; her dark eyes showing that wistful look that I had learned to watch for. The corners of her red mouth drooped a little, and she looked like a tired child who ought to be protected and cared for against all misfortune.

"I thought George would come up this afternoon," she said, as she stood looking idly out of the window, where her slight black-robed figure made a lovely picture against the background of the gold-colored silk curtain.

"I'm glad he didn't," I said involuntarily; "I'm glad to have you to myself."

She looked up startled, for I never before expressed a hint of my personal feeling toward her. What she read in my eyes must have been intelligible to her, for her own lids dropped, and a soft pink blush showed faintly on her pale cheeks.

"Do you mind that I want you to myself?" I said, going to her side.

"No," she replied and again she gave me a fleeting glance that proved her not entirely unconscious of my meaning, and not offended by it.

"Janet," I went on, taking both her hands in mine, "it may seem dreadful to tell you now, when I've known you but a few days, but I must tell you that I love you. You know it, of course, and believe me, dear, I'm not asking you to respond,—yet. Just let me love you now, until this wretched business is finished, and then, after that, let me teach you to love me."

"It's too late for you to do that," she whispered, and then, overcome with this sudden knowledge, I clasped her in my arms and realized the meaning of the tenderness in her eyes and the wistful droop of her scarlet lips.

"You darling," I murmured, as I held her close; "you precious, contradictory bit of feminine humanity! This is the most blessed of all your contradictions, for I never dreamed that you already loved me."

"But you can't doubt it now, can you?" she returned, as she rested, contentedly, in my embrace.

"No, dearest, you are not easy to understand, there is much about your nature that puzzles me, but when that true, sincere look comes into your eyes, I know you are in earnest. Oh, Janet, my darling, how happy we shall be after all this troublesome mystery is cleared up, and you and I can devote our whole life to caring for each other."

"I shall be so glad to be happy," she said, with a wistful little sigh, and I remembered that her life, so far, had given her little or no joy.

"Sweetheart," I said, "my life purpose henceforth shall be to give you happiness enough to make up for the sad years you have spent.

"You can easily do that, my dear," and the tenderness in her eyes fairly transfigured her. And then, with a pretty impetuous gesture, she hid her face on my shoulder.

"But it doesn't seem possible," I said, after a time, "that you can really love me when you've known me but a few days."

"That doesn't count in a love like ours," said Janet, speaking almost solemnly. "It is not the kind that requires time to grow."

"No," I agreed, "it was born full grown. I always told Laura that when I fell in love it would be at first sight, and it was. The marvellous part, dear, is that you care, too."

"Care!" she exclaimed, and the depths of love in her eyes gave me a hint of her emotional nature; "but," she went on, "this is all wrong. You must not talk to me like this, and I must not listen to it. I am under suspicion of having committed a crime. Surely you cannot love me until I am freed from that."

"But you are not guilty?"

I asked the question not because of any doubt in my own mind, but because I wanted for once to hear her own statement of her innocence.

"That I shall not tell you," she said, and her eyes took on a faraway, inscrutable look, as of a sphinx; "that you must find out for yourself. Or rather, no, I don't want you to find out. I want it always to remain a mystery."

"What, Janet! you don't want me to find out who killed your uncle!"

"Oh, no, no!" and her voice rang out in agonized entreaty; "please don't, Otis; please don't try to find out who did it!"

"But then, dear, how can you be freed from suspicion? and I want to tell you, Janet, I want to tell you now, while I hold you in my arms,—I want to tell you in the same breath that I tell you of my love,—that you will be accused of this crime, unless the real criminal is discovered."

"How do you know I'm not the real criminal?"

"I know it for two reasons. First, because I love you, and I'm telling you so; and second, because you love me, and——"

"I'm not telling you so," she interrupted, and a look of pain came into her dear eyes as she tried to resist my embrace.

"You don't have to tell me, dear," I said, quietly, "I know it. But you must tell me who it is that you are trying to shield by your strange ways and words. Is it Leroy? It can't be Charlotte."

"I'm not shielding anybody," she cried out; "the jury people proved that I must have killed Uncle Robert myself, and so, you see, I must have done so."

"Now you're talking childishly," I said, as I soothed her, gently; "of course you didn't kill him, darling; but you do know more about it than you have yet told, and you must tell me, because I'm going to save you from any further unpleasantness. I wish I could understand you, you bewitching mystery! You are surely shielding some one. It can't be that absurd J. S. I hardly think it can be the man of the handkerchief; oh, but I haven't told you about that yet. It can't be George,—because he has a perfect alibi."

"I suppose if it were not for that alibi, George might be suspected," said Janet slowly.

"Indeed he might, but as there are people to swear to his presence in another part of town at the time of the crime, he is beyond suspicion. I wish you had such an alibi, dearest."

"Oh, I wish I did! Otis, what do you think? You know I was locked in that house and nobody could get in. You know I didn't kill Uncle Robert. Now who did?"

"Janet," I said, very seriously, "I don't know. And I have nearly lost hope of finding out. So I will tell you what I have decided to do; I'm going to consult Fleming Stone."

"Fleming Stone? Who is he?"

"He is probably the cleverest detective in the city. I feel sure that he can solve our mystery, if he will undertake it."

"Oh, don't have a detective!" she cried; "at least, not that Mr. Stone. He can find out everything!"

"And don't you want everything found out?" I asked, looking at her intently.

"No!" she cried vehemently. "I don't! I want Uncle Robert's death always to remain a mystery!"

"It can't be a greater mystery than you are!" I exclaimed, for the words were wrung from me as I looked at the girl's face, which had again taken on that white, impassive look.

133

It was at that moment that Laura returned, and as she entered the library, Janet fled away to her own room.

Laura looked at me questioningly, and I told her quite frankly all that had passed between Janet and myself.

She kissed me tenderly, like the dear sister that she is, and said; "Don't worry, Otis; it will come out all right. I know Janet much better than you do. She is innocent, of course, but she is so unnerved and distraught with these dreadful days, that I'm only surprised she bears up as well as she does. Leave her to me, and you go and get your Fleming Stone, and use every effort to persuade him to take the case."

As it had been my life-long habit to take Laura's advice, especially when it coincided with my own inclination I started off at once to hunt up Fleming Stone.

I knew the man slightly, having run across him a few times in a business way, and I knew that not only were his services exceedingly high-priced, but also that he never took any case unless of great difficulty and peculiar interest. I hoped, however, that the circumstances of the Pembroke affair would appeal to him, and I determined to use every effort to interest him in it.

By good fortune, I found him at home, and willing to listen to a statement of my business.

Fleming Stone's personality was not at all of the taciturn, inscrutable variety. He was a large man, of genial and charming manner, and possessed of a personal magnetism that seemed to invite confidence and confidences. I knew him well enough to know that if I could win his interest at all it would be by a brief statement of the mystery as a puzzle, and a request that he help me solve it.

"Mr. Stone," I began, "if three persons spent the night in an apartment so securely locked on the inside that there was no possible means of ingress, and if in the morning it was found that one of those three persons had been murdered at midnight, would you say that the guilt must rest upon either one or both of the other two persons?"

At any rate, I had succeeded in catching the man's attention.

As there was no question of personal feeling in my statement, he seemed to look at it as an abstract problem, and replied at once:

"According to the facts as you have stated them, the guilt must necessarily rest upon one or both of the other two persons. But this is assuming that it really was a murder, that there really was no mode of ingress, and that there really were no other persons in the apartment."

Having secured Fleming Stone's interest in the abstract

134

statement, I proceeded to lay before him the concrete story of the Pembroke affair.

He listened gravely, asking only one or two questions, and when I had told him all I knew about it he sat thinking for a few moments.

At last, unable to control my impatience, I said: "Do you now think the guilt rests upon either one or both of those women?"

As I have said, Mr. Stone was not of the secretive and close-mouthed style of detective, and he said in his frank and pleasant way: "Not necessarily, by any means. Indeed, from what you have told me, I should say that the two women knew nothing about the crime until the morning. But this, of course, is a mere surmise, based on your account of the case."

As I had told him the facts as I knew them, with all their horrible incrimination of Janet, I was greatly relieved at his words.

"Then," said I, "will you take up the case, and find the criminal as soon as may be? Money is no object, but time is precious, as I strongly desire to avoid any possibility of a trial of Miss Pembroke."

"Have you any other clues other than those you have told me?"

"I haven't told you any," I said, in some surprise; "but we certainly have several."

He listened with the greatest attention, while I told him in rapid succession of the key, the time-table, the ticket stubs, the torn telegram, the handkerchief, and finally, the missing money.

"Have you traced these to their sources?" he inquired.

"We have, and each one led to a different man."

I then told him of Jonathan Scudder, of Graham Leroy, of James Decker, and of William Sydney Gresham, and he listened with a half-smile on his pleasant, responsive face.

"Of course you can see all these clues for yourself," I went on, "and I feel sure, Mr. Stone, that by an examination of them, you can deduce much of the personality of the criminal."

"I don't care to see them," was his astonishing answer; "I have already deduced from them the evidence that they clearly show."

"Your statement would amaze me," I said, "except that I had resolved not to be surprised at anything you might say or do, for I know your methods are mysterious and your powers little short of miraculous."

"Don't credit me with supernatural ability, Mr. Landon," said Stone, smiling genially. "Let me compliment you on the graphic way in which you have described that collection of clues. I can fairly see them, in my mind's eye lying before me. Were not the ticket stubs bent and broken and a good deal soiled?"

"They were," I said, staring at him.

135

"And was the time-table smudged with dirt, and perhaps bearing an impress of tiny dots in regular rows?"

"Now I know you're a wizard!" I exclaimed, "for that's exactly what I did see! such a mark on the first page of that time-table!"

"It might easily not have been there," said Stone, musingly; "I confess I chanced that. It was merely a hazard, but it helps. Yes, Mr. Landon, your collection of clues is indeed valuable and of decided assistance in discovering the identity of the person or persons unknown."

It struck a chill to my heart that Fleming Stone seemed to avoid the use of a masculine pronoun. Could he, too, think that a woman was implicated, and if not, why didn't he say the man who committed the crime, instead of dodging behind the vague term he had used. With a desperate idea of forcing this point, I said; "The Coroner believes that since the weapon used was a hat-pin, the criminal was a woman."

"Why did you say it was a hat-pin?" said Fleming Stone, and I realized that his brain was already busy with the subtleties of the case.

"The doctors stated that it was part of a hat-pin, the other end of which had been broken off."

"Did you see the pin that was extracted from the wound?"

"I did."

"How long was it?"

"Almost exactly four inches."

"And are you prepared to affirm that it is part of a hat-pin, and not a complete pin of a shorter length?"

"I am not. The thought did not before occur to me. But as it had no head on it, we assumed that it was probably the half of a broken hat-pin. It is by no means the first instance on record of using a hat-pin as a murderous weapon."

"No," said Fleming Stone; "and yet that does not prove it a hat-pin. May it not have been a shawl-pin, or some shorter pin that women use in their costumes?"

"It may have been," said I; "but women do not wear shawls nowadays. At any rate, any pin of that length would seem to indicate a woman's crime."

"Well, as a rule," said Fleming Stone, smiling, "we men do not pin our garments together; but I dare say almost any man, if he wanted one, could gain possession of such a pin."

How true this was, and how foolish we had been to assume that a woman's pin must have meant a woman's crime! A picture passed through my mind of Laura's dressing-table, where I could have procured any kind of a pin, with no trouble whatever.

"Moreover," went on Fleming Stone, "the great majority of hat-pins used in America will not break. They will bend, as they are usually made of iron, though occasionally of steel."

I looked at the man with growing admiration. How widespread was his knowledge, and how logical his deduction!

"I should have to see the pin," said Stone, "before drawing any conclusion from it. You did not examine it closely, you say?"

I had not said so, but I suppose he deduced it from my slight knowledge of its characteristics.

"I did not examine it through a microscope," I replied.

"You should have done so. If it were really a broken hat-pin, it would show a clean, bright break at the end; whereas, were it a shorter pin which had lost its head, it would show at the end a fraction of an inch of duller steel, and perhaps an irregular surface where the head had been attached."

"I can see that you are right, but I cannot see why it should make much difference which it was."

"My dear sir, according to your statement, the only clue we have to work upon is the weapon which was used. The weapon is always an important item, if not the most important, and it cannot be scrutinized too closely or examined too minutely, for, sooner or later, it is almost always certain to expose the criminal."

"I had thought," I said humbly, "that I possessed a degree of detective instinct, but I now see I was mistaken. I assumed the pin to be a hat-pin, and thought no more about it."

"It may be one," said Stone, "and the only way to find out is to see it. Of course I must also examine the apartment, and then, if necessary, question some of the parties concerned. But at this moment I have little doubt in my mind as to who killed Robert Pembroke. I will take the case, because, though unusual, it promises to be a short one. I think I may safely say that by to-morrow night at this hour we will not only have discovered the criminal, but obtained a confession. But I will say the criminal has been very, very clever. In fact, I think I should never have conceived of such various kinds of cleverness combined in one crime. But, as is often the case, he has outwitted himself. His very cleverness is his undoing."

Surely the man was a wizard! I looked at him without a word after he had made his astounding announcement. I had no idea whom he suspected, but I knew he would not tell me if I asked, so I thought best to express no curiosity, but to leave the matter in his hands, and await his further pleasure.

"You can go at once to see the apartment," I said; "but to look at the pin we shall have to wait until morning, as I think it is in charge of the coroner."

"It must all wait till morning," said Fleming Stone, "as I have other work that I must attend to this evening."

I accepted my dismissal, and, making an appointment to call for him the next day, I turned my steps homeward.

I had purposely said nothing to Fleming Stone of my suspicion of George Lawrence. Indeed, it was scarcely strong enough to be called a suspicion, and, too, the mere idea of his going into the apartment implied the idea of his being let in by Janet. Therefore, I had contended myself with telling Stone the facts as I knew them, and suppressing my own opinion. Also, it seemed a dreadful thing to cast suspicion on Lawrence, when I had no evidence of any sort.

XXII

A CALL ON MISS WARING

When I arose next morning I assured myself that I was in all probability the happiest man in the city. With Fleming Stone's assurance that that very night should see the Pembroke mystery cleared up, and with the knowledge in my heart that Janet loved me, I felt that my future outlook was little less than glorious.

I had given up all ambition to be a detective; I even had little care as to the outcome of Fleming Stone's investigation—granting, of course, that Janet and George were in no way implicated. I could have given myself up to the happy dreams which are usually said to be indulged in by men of fewer years than my own, but I remembered my appointment and hastened away to meet Fleming Stone.

Though I had a vague feeling of fear as to the result of this day's work, yet I knew it must be gone through with, and I prepared to face whatever might be before me.

Together we went to the District Attorney's office.

Mr. Buckner was much impressed by the fact of Fleming Stone's connection with the case, for it was well known that the great detective accepted only puzzling problems. It was quite evident, however, that the District Attorney could see no reason for more than one opinion as to the Pembroke tragedy.

"Here are the clues," said Mr. Buckner, as he arranged the collection on his desk.

The torn telegram was not among them, and I realized that Buckner had excluded that, because the letter from Jonathan Scudder practically denied it.

Fleming Stone glanced at the key and the handkerchief with the briefest attention. He picked up the ticket stubs and the time-table, but after a moment's scrutiny he laid them down again, murmuring, as if to himself, "Clever, very clever!"

"Mr. Buckner," he said at last, "these clues seem to me all to point to the same criminal, and a most ingenious person as well."

"You speak in riddles, Mr. Stone," said the District Attorney, "I confess I thought these articles of but slight importance, as they have been traced each to a different owner."

"Even so," said Stone, "they are distinctly indicative, and form a large share of the evidence piling up against the criminal. But a far more important clue is the weapon with which Mr. Pembroke was killed. Will you show me that?"

Buckner took the pin from a drawer and offered it to Mr. Stone, saying, "There is the weapon. If the head of the hat-pin had been left on, it might be traced to the woman who used it. But as she broke it off, this small portion cannot be traced. She doubtless broke the head off purposely, thus proving herself, as you have already remarked, Mr. Stone, a very clever criminal."

Mr. Stone took the pin, glanced at it a moment, and then, taking a magnifying-glass from his pocket, examined it carefully.

"It is not a hat-pin," he said, "nor is it part of a hat-pin. The pin as you see it there is its full length. The head has been removed, not accidentally, but purposely. It had been removed, and carefully, before the pin was used as a weapon."

"May I ask how you know this, sir?" asked the coroner respectfully.

"Certainly," said Stone, in his affable way. "If you will look at the end of the pin through this glass, you will see unmistakable signs that the head has been removed. For about an eighth of an inch you note a slight discoloration, caused by the attaching of the glass head. You also see on one side a minute portion of glass still adhering to the steel. Had the head been accidentally or carelessly broken off, it is probable that more glass would have adhered to the pin. The head was therefore purposely and carefully removed, perhaps by smashing it with something heavy or by stepping on it. The fragment of glass that is attached to the pin is, as you may see if you will hold it up to the light, of a violet color. The pin, therefore, I'm prepared to assert, is one of the pins which first-class florists give away with bunches of violets bought at their shops. I have never seen these pins with violet-colored heads used for any other purpose, though it is not impossible that they may be. I say a first-class florist, because it is only they who use this style of pin; the smaller shops give black-headed ones. But the larger flower dealers make a specialty of using purple tin-foil for their violet bunches, tying them with purple cord or ribbon, and placing them in a purple pasteboard box. To harmonize with this color scheme, they have of late years provided these violet-headed flower pins. All this is of importance in our quest, for it ought to be easier to trace a violet pin than the more universally used hat-pin."

How different Fleming Stone's manner from the bumptious and know-it-all air of the average detective! He was quite willing to share any information which he gained, and seemed to treat his fellow-workers as his equals in perspicacity and cleverness.

We had learned something, to be sure. But as the coroner had no other objects of evidence to show us, and there seemed nothing more to be learned from the pin, Fleming Stone turned into the street, and I followed him.

"Could not the head have been broken off after the pin was used to commit the murder?" I inquired.

"No," said Stone; "it would be impossible to break off a glass head with one's fingers under such conditions. It could have been done by some instrument, but that is not likely. And then, too, there would probably have been bits of glass on the pillow."

"Bits of glass!" I exclaimed. "Bits of violet-colored glass! Why, man alive, I have them in my pocket now!"

"Let me see them," said Stone. "It may save us quite a search."

It took more to excite Fleming Stone's enthusiasm than it did mine, and he seemed almost unaware of the importance of my statement; but when I took a white paper from my pocket, unfolded it, and showed him the specks of glass I had found in Lawrence's apartment the night before, his flashing eyes showed that he thought it indeed a clue. But he only said quietly: "You should have mentioned this in your statement of the case. Why did you not?"

"The real reason is that I forgot it," I admitted, frankly. "But I had no idea it was important evidence, for I never dreamed these bits could be the head of a pin. I thought them a portion of a broken bottle. You know druggists use small phials of that color for certain prescriptions."

"Some druggists use bottles of this color for poison," said Fleming Stone, "but that doesn't affect our case, for Mr. Pembroke was not poisoned. But it may easily be the head of the pin we were talking about. Where did you find this glass?"

"In George Lawrence's studio," I replied, looking a little shamefaced at my own obvious stupidity.

"Well, you are a clever detective!" said Fleming Stone; but so genial was the smile of mild amusement he turned upon me, that I could not feel hurt at his sarcasm.

"You didn't even tell me that you examined young Lawrence's studio, and you haven't yet told me why you did so. I assume you have no intent to conceal anything from me."

"I have not," I said. "I'm mortified—first that I did not realize the importance of this broken glass, and next because I didn't mention the incident to you. It was a stupid blunder of mine, but I assure you it was not intentional."

"It may mean much, and it may mean nothing," said Fleming Stone, "but it must be investigated. Where, in the studio, was the glass?"

"On the marble hearthstone," said I.

141

"Where it might easily have been broken off the pin by a boot heel, or other means. But we must not assume more than the evidence clearly indicates. Tell me more of young Lawrence. Was he what is known as a ladies' man? Would he be likely to take bunches of violets to his feminine friends?"

"I know the man very slightly," I answered, "but I should judge him to be rather attentive to the fair sex. Indeed, I know that the day before yesterday he escorted a young lady to a matinée, and that night he dined and spent the evening at the home of the same girl."

"Do you know this young lady?" he asked.

"I know her name," I replied. "It is Miss Waring, and she lives in Sixtieth Street."

"And your own home is in Sixty-second Street?"

"Yes. If necessary, I can telephone to my sister, and she will ask Miss Pembroke for Miss Waring's address."

"Do so," said Fleming Stone; and I knew from the gravity of his expression that he was rapidly constructing a serious case against somebody.

I obtained the desired information over the telephone, and then, with Fleming Stone, boarded a car going uptown. Though still pleasant-mannered and responsive, Stone seemed disinclined to talk, so the journey was made almost in silence.

When we reached Miss Waring's, Mr. Stone sent up his card, asking her to grant him an interview as soon as possible.

In a few moments Millicent Waring appeared. She was a dainty little blonde, with what is known as a society manner, though not marked by foolish affectation.

Fleming Stone introduced himself and then introduced me, in a pleasant way, and with a politeness that would have been admired by the most punctilious of critics.

"Pray do not be alarmed, Miss Waring," he began, "at the legal aspect of your callers."

"Not at all," said the girl, smiling prettily. "I am pleased to meet one of whom I have always stood in awe, and to discover that in appearance, at least, he is not a bit awe-inspiring."

Whether Miss Waring was always so self-poised and at her ease, or whether it was Fleming Stone's magnetic manner that made her appear so, I did not know, but the two were soon chatting like old friends. My part, apparently, was merely that of a listener, and I was well content that it should be so.

"You know Mr. Lawrence?" Mr. Stone was saying. "Mr. George Lawrence?"

"Oh, yes," said the girl; "and I have read in the paper of a dreadful tragedy in his family."

142

"Yes; his uncle, I believe. You have seen Mr. Lawrence recently, Miss Waring?"

"Last Wednesday I went with him to a matinée. After the theatre he brought me back here. Then he went home, but he came back here to dinner and spent the evening."

"At what time did he leave?"

"At eleven o'clock precisely."

"How do you know the time so accurately?"

"Because as he came to say good-night I was standing near the mantel, where there is a small French clock. It struck the hour, and I remember his remarking on the sweet tone of the chime, and he counted the strokes to eleven. He then went away at once."

"You mean he left the drawing-room?"

"Yes; and a moment later I saw him pass through the hall, and he nodded in at me as he passed the drawing-room door on his way out. Why are you asking me all this? But I suppose it is part of the red tape in connection with the dreadful affair."

"Is Mr. Lawrence a particular friend of yours? You must pardon the question, Miss Waring, but you also must answer it." Fleming Stone's smile robbed the words of any hint of rudeness.

"Oh, dear, no!" said Miss Waring, laughing gaily; "that is, I like him, you know, and he's awfully kind and polite to me, but he's merely an acquaintance."

"Did you go anywhere on your way to and from the theatre?"

"No, I think not—oh, yes, we did, too; just before we went into the theatre Mr. Lawrence insisted on stopping at the florist's for some violets. He said no matinée girl was complete without a bunch of violets."

"And did you pin them on your gown?" asked Stone, as if in a most casual way.

"No, indeed," said Miss Waring; "I never do that. It spoils a nice gown to pin flowers on it."

"And what did you do with the pin?"

"What pin?"

"The pin that a florist always gives you with violets."

"Oh, yes, those purple-headed pins. Why, I don't know what I did do with it." The girl's pretty brow wrinkled in her endeavor to remember, and then cleared as she said: "Oh, yes, it comes back to me now! When I said I wouldn't use it, lest the flowers should spoil my gown, I handed it to Mr. Lawrence, and he stuck it in his coat lapel—underneath, you know—for, he said, perhaps I might change my mind. But, of course, I didn't, and I'm sure I don't know what became of the pin. Do you want one? I have dozens of them up-stairs."

"No," said Fleming Stone; "and I don't think we need encroach further on your time, Miss Waring. I thank you for your goodness in seeing us, and I would like to ask you to say nothing about this interview for twenty-four hours. After that you need not consider it confidential."

I believe Fleming Stone's manner would have wheedled a promise out of the Egyptian Sphinx, and I was not in the least surprised to hear Miss Waring agree to his stipulations.

When we again reached the street Fleming Stone observed: "Without going so far as to designate our attitude toward George Lawrence by the word 'suspicion,' we must admit that the young man had a motive, and, that there is evidence whether true or not, to indicate his having had in his possession a weapon at least similar to the one used."

The doubt I had felt all along of Lawrence was, of course, strengthened by Miss Waring's disclosures; but to have George accused was only one degree less awful than to have suspicion cast on Janet. And, too, notwithstanding the strange and somewhat complicated evidence of the violet pin, Lawrence had told me he had a perfect alibi. And then, besides this, how could he have gained entrance to the apartment at the dead of night, unless Janet had let him in? I could not bring up this last point, lest Fleming Stone should immediately deduce Janet's complicity; but I would learn how he proposed to prove George's guilt when George was able to prove his presence at another place at the time of the fatal deed.

"But," I said, "evidence is of little use so far as Mr. Lawrence is concerned, for he has a perfect alibi."

XXIII

LAWRENCE'S STATEMENT

To my surprise, instead of seeming baffled by my statement, Fleming Stone gave me a quizzical glance.

"A perfect alibi?" he repeated. "How do you know?"

"He told me so," I said confidently.

"Why did he tell you that? Did he expect to be accused?"

"No," I replied; "I do not think he did. You know, Mr. Stone, I never met young Lawrence till since this affair; but, unless I am no judge of human nature, he is a frank, honest sort of chap, with a whole lot of common sense, and he said to his cousin, in my presence, that in the course of legal proceedings he might easily be called upon to give an account of his own movements the night of the murder, but that he was prepared to prove a perfect alibi. Therefore, you see, we cannot suspect him, notwithstanding the coincidence of the violet-colored glass."

"He can prove a perfect alibi," again repeated Fleming Stone, and again that strange little gleam of satisfaction crept into his eyes. It irritated while it fascinated me, and I wondered in what direction his suspicions would next turn.

"Did he tell you," he asked, "the nature of this alibi?"

I was struck with a sudden thought. For some reason, the detective even yet suspected George, and all I said seemed to strengthen rather than allay his suspicion. I would, therefore, give the suspected man a chance to speak for himself.

"He did," I answered; "but instead of repeating to you at secondhand what he told me, would it not be better to go down to his place and let him tell it for himself?"

"Very much better," said Stone heartily; and again we started downtown. It was well on toward noon, and it seemed to me we had made no definite progress. After Fleming Stone had told me he would discover the criminal that day, I couldn't help imagining a sudden bringing to book of some burly ruffian whose face was well known in the rogues' gallery, but unfamiliar to those in my walk of life. But Stone's sudden interest in George Lawrence filled me with a vague fear that the trail he was evidently following might somehow implicate Janet before he had finished. However, as I was feeling convinced that George's own testimony would affect Fleming Stone more favorably than my own version of it, I felt glad indeed that we were bound on our present errand.

And so we came again to the house in Washington Square where Lawrence lived.

The young man was at home, and received us in his studio. He seemed no whit embarrassed at the detective's visit, greeted me pleasantly, and expressed himself as quite willing to tell us anything we wanted to know.

"Of course you understand," began Fleming Stone, "that with so few possible witnesses, it is necessary to make a somewhat thorough examination of each one."

"Certainly," said George, whose own affability of manner quite equalled that of the celebrated detective.

"Then," went on Stone, "I will ask you, if you please, to detail your own occupations on last Wednesday."

"Beginning in the morning?" asked George.

"If you please."

"Well, let me see. I didn't get up very early, and after I did rise I stayed around here in my studio until luncheon time. During the morning I worked on several sketches for a book I am doing. About twelve o'clock I went uptown and lunched with a friend, a fellow-artist, at a little German restaurant. After that I went and called for Miss Millicent Waring, whom I had invited to go with me to a matinée. I had expected Mrs. Waring to accompany us, but as she was ill she allowed Miss Waring to go with me alone, although it is not Miss Waring's habit to go about unchaperoned."

I couldn't help feeling a certain satisfaction in listening to young Lawrence's story. I was glad that his habits and his friends were all so correct and so entirely free from the unconventionality which is sometimes noticed in the social doings of young artists.

"We went to the matinée," continued George, "in Mrs. Waring's carriage, which also came for us, after the performance."

"One moment," said Fleming Stone. "You stopped nowhere, going or coming?"

"No," said Lawrence; "nowhere."

"Except at the florist's," observed Stone quietly.

It may have been my imagination, but I thought that George started at these words. However, he said in a cool, steady voice:

"Ah, yes, I had forgotten that. We stopped a moment to get some violets for Miss Waring."

"And after the matinée you drove home with Miss Waring?"

"Yes," said Lawrence; "and left her at her own door. She invited me to come back to dinner, and I said I would. As the Warings' house is only two blocks away from the Pembroke's, I thought I would run in for a few moments to see Janet. I did this, and Janet seemed glad to see me, but Uncle Robert was so crusty and irritable

146

that I did not care to stay very long. I left there about six, came back here to my room, and dressed for dinner. From here I went directly back to the Warings', reaching there at 7.30, which was the dinner hour. There were other guests, and after dinner there was music in the drawing-room. I stayed until eleven o'clock. As I said good-night to Miss Waring, the clock chanced to be striking eleven, so I'm sure of the time. From the Warings' I came right back here on a Broadway car. I reached this house at 11.25, it having taken me about twenty-five minutes to come down from Sixtieth Street and to walk over here from Broadway."

"How do you know you reached this house at exactly 11.25?" Fleming Stone asked this with such an air of cordial interest that there was no trace of cross-questioning about it.

"Because," said George easily, "my watch had stopped—it had run down during the evening—and so as I came into this house I asked the hall boy what time it was, that I might set my watch. He looked at the office clock, and told me. Of course you can verify this by the boy."

"I've no desire to verify your statement, Mr. Lawrence," said Stone, with his winning smile. "It's a bad habit, this letting a watch run down. Do you often do it?"

"No," said Lawrence; "almost never. Indeed, I don't know when it has happened before."

"And then what next, Mr. Lawrence?"

"Then the hall boy brought me up in the elevator, I let myself into my rooms, and went at once to bed."

"Then the first intimation of your uncle's death you received the next morning?"

"Yes, when Janet telephoned to me. But she didn't say Uncle Robert was dead. She merely asked me to come up there at once, and I went."

"What did you think she wanted you for?"

"I thought that either uncle was ill or she was herself, for she had never telephoned for me before in the morning."

"I thank you, Mr. Lawrence," said Fleming Stone, "for your frank and straightforward account of this affair, and for your courteous answers to my questions. You know, of course, that it is the unpleasant duty of a detective to ask questions unmercifully, in the hope of being set upon the right track at last."

"I quite appreciate your position, my dear sir, and I trust I have given you all the information you desire. As I have told Mr. Landon, I have no taste for detective work myself, but I suppose it has to be done by somebody."

After polite good-byes on both sides, we left Lawrence in his studio, and went down-stairs. Mr. Stone insisted on walking down, though it was four flights, and I, of course, raised no objection.

When we reached the ground floor he stepped into the office, which was a small room just at the right of the entrance, and not far from the elevator.

After a glance at the office clock which stood on the desk, Mr. Stone addressed himself to the office boy.

"Do you remember," he said, "that Mr. Lawrence came in here last Wednesday night?"

"Yes, sir," said the boy; "I do."

"At what time was it?"

"Just twenty-five minutes after eleven, sir."

"How can you fix the time so exactly, my boy?"

"Because when Mr. Lawrence came in, his watch had stopped, and he asked me what time it was by the office clock."

"Couldn't he see for himself?"

"I suppose he could, sir, but, any way, he asked me, and I told him; and then I took him up in the elevator, and he was setting his watch on the way up. Just before he got out he said: 'Did you say 11.25?' and I said, 'Yes.'"

"The office clock is always about right, I suppose?" said Mr. Stone, and, taking his watch from his pocket, he compared the two. There was but a minute's difference.

"Yes, sir, just about right; but that night I thought it was later when Mr. Lawrence come in. I was surprised myself when I see it wasn't half past eleven yet. But, of course, I must have made a mistake, for this clock is never more than a couple of minutes out of the way."

"What time does your elevator stop running?"

"Not at all, sir, we run it all night."

"And other men came in after Mr. Lawrence did that night?"

"Oh, yes, sir; lots of them. These is bachelor apartments, you know, and the men come in quite late—sometimes up till two or three o'clock."

Apparently Fleming Stone had learned all he wanted to know from the boy, and after he had thanked him and had also slipped into his hand a bit of more material reward, the interview was at an end.

We went out into the street again, and Fleming Stone said: "Now I should like to examine the Pembrokes' apartment."

"And shall you want to interview Miss Pembroke?" I inquired.

"Yes, I think so," he replied; "but we will look over the apartment first."

"We'll have something to eat first," I declared; "and if you'll

148

come home with me, I'll guarantee that my sister will give you quite as satisfactory a luncheon as you could obtain in the best hotel in the city."

"I've no doubt of it," said Stone pleasantly; "and I accept your invitation with pleasure. Will you wait for me a minute, while I telephone?"

Before I had time to reply he had slipped in through a doorway at which hung the familiar blue sign.

In a minute or two he rejoined me, and said: "Now let's dismiss the whole affair from our minds until after luncheon. It is never wise to let business interfere with digestion."

As we rode up home in the car, Mr. Stone was most agreeable and entertaining. Not a word was said of the Pembroke case—he seemed really to have laid aside all thought of it—and yet I couldn't help a sinister conviction that when he telephoned it had been a message to headquarters, authorizing the surveillance, if not the arrest, of somebody. It couldn't be Lawrence, in the face of that alibi; it couldn't be Janet, for he knew next to nothing about her connection with the matter; it couldn't be Charlotte, of course; and so it must have been "some person or persons unknown" to me.

I felt no hesitancy, so far as Laura was concerned, in taking home an unexpected guest, for it was my habit to do that whenever I chose, and I had never found Laura otherwise than pleased to see my friends, and amply able to provide hospitality for them. But, as we neared the house, I remembered Janet's strange disinclination to employ a detective, and her apparent horror at the mention of Fleming Stone's name.

Feeling that honesty demanded it, I told Fleming Stone exactly what Janet had said on this subject when I had left the house that morning. Though apparently not disturbed personally by Miss Pembroke's attitude toward him, he seemed to consider it as of definite importance for some other reason.

"Why should Miss Pembroke object to a detective's services," he said, "when, as you have told me, Mr. Lawrence said at your dinner table last night that he wanted to engage the best possible detective skill?"

"I don't know," I replied. "I'm puzzled myself. But I admit, Mr. Stone, that Miss Pembroke has been an enigma to me from the first. Not only do I believe her innocent, but I have a warmer regard for her than I am perhaps justified in mentioning to a stranger; and yet she is so contradictory in her speech and action from time to time that I simply do not know what to think."

Fleming Stone turned a very kind glance on me. "The hardest puzzle in this world," he said, "is a woman. Of course I do not know

149

Miss Pembroke, but I hope she will consent to meet me, notwithstanding her aversion to detectives."

"I think she will," I said; "and, besides, she is so changeable that at this moment she may be more anxious to see a detective than anybody else."

"Let us hope so," he said somewhat gravely. "It may be much to her advantage."

XXIV

THE CHAIN OF EVIDENCE

Laura greeted us cordially; and Miss Pembroke, with a politeness which, though slightly constrained, was quiet and non-committal. But, as I had hoped, Fleming Stone's winning manner and charming conversational ability seemed to make Janet forget her aversion to detectives. At the luncheon table various subjects were touched upon, but it was not long before we drifted into a discussion of the theme uppermost in all our minds. I could see that although Fleming Stone was apparently talking in a casual way, he was closely studying Janet's face as he talked.

I noticed that when any reference was made to George Lawrence, Janet seemed perturbed, and, although Mr. Stone said flatly that George could not have entered when the door was chained, this did not seem to lessen Janet's concern. But when Stone referred to George's perfect alibi, Janet looked relieved, as if freed from a great fear.

It was entirely due to Fleming Stone's tact that the conversation was kept at a light and airy level. I was intensely conscious of a growing portent of evil. A cloak of gloom seemed to be settling around me, and it was only with the utmost effort that I could control my nervous apprehensions. What was going to happen, I did not know, but I felt intuitively that a climax was fast approaching, and at last I found myself sacrificing all other sympathies to the hope that Janet might be spared.

I could see that Laura was equally agitated, although she too was outwardly calm. Janet, as always, was a puzzle. She seemed alternately depressed or gladdened in proportion as the drift of suspicion seemed directed toward or away from her cousin George.

In a word, Fleming Stone's personality dominated us all. We were but as strings of an instrument upon which he played, and we responded involuntarily to his impulses or at his will.

Into this surcharged atmosphere came another element with the entrance of George Lawrence. He looked handsome and debonair as usual, and informally begged of Mrs. Mulford permission to share our after-dinner coffee.

"We're glad to have you," said Laura, in her affable way, "and, as we have finished luncheon, we will have our coffee in the library, where we can be more comfortable."

Although Lawrence seemed perfectly at ease, and unconscious

of any reason to fear Fleming Stone's investigations, I couldn't help feeling that his air of ease was assumed. It was not so much any signs of nervousness or sensitiveness about him, as it was the pronounced absence of these. It seemed to me that he was playing a part of straightforward fearlessness, but was slightly overdoing it.

Fleming Stone talked to Lawrence casually, referring once to his perfect alibi. George remarked that though he had no fear of suspicion falling in his direction, it gave him a feeling of satisfaction to know that he could satisfactorily account for his whereabouts at the time the murder was committed.

"And now," said Mr. Stone, after the coffee service had been removed, "I think I will make my examination of the apartment opposite. It is not probable that I will discover anything in the nature of a clue, but as a detective I certainly must examine the scene of the crime. I would prefer to go alone, if you will give a key. I will rejoin you here after my search."

Janet gave Mr. Stone her key, and without further word he crossed the hall alone to what had been the Pembrokes' apartment.

After Fleming Stone's departure a strange chill fell on the mental atmosphere of our little party. George Lawrence seemed to lose his careless air, and a grayish pallor settled on his face, notwithstanding his apparent effort to appear as usual. Janet watched her cousin closely, and she herself seemed on the verge of nervous collapse. Laura, like the blessed woman she is, strove bravely to keep up, but I saw that she too felt that the end was near. As for myself, remembering Fleming Stone's promise, I seemed to be possessed, to the exclusion of all else, of a great fear for Janet.

It could not have been more than ten minutes, if as much as that, before Fleming Stone returned.

As he entered our library he seemed to have lost his professional aspect, and I thought I had never seen a sadder or more sympathetic expression than I read in his eyes.

"Mr. Lawrence," he said, without preamble, "it is my duty to arrest you for the murder of your uncle, Robert Pembroke."

For a moment there was no sound, and then, with a pathetic, heart-breaking little cry, Janet said: "Oh, I hoped so that it wasn't you!"

To my surprise, Lawrence tried to deny it. Guilt seemed to me to be written in every line of his face, yet, with a palpable effort, he assumed an air of bravado and said: "I told you I might be accused, but I can prove a perfect alibi."

"Mr. Lawrence," said Fleming Stone, more sternly than he had yet spoken, "you have over-reached yourself. That very phrase, 'I can prove a perfect alibi,' gave me the first hint that your alibi was a manufactured one. An innocent man can rarely prove a perfect alibi. Not one man in a hundred can give accurate account to the minute of his goings and comings. Your alibi is too perfect; its very perfection is its flaw. Again, the idea of proving an alibi, or, rather, the idea of using that phrase, would not occur to an honest man. He would know that circumstances must prove his alibi. It was that which proved to me that Mr. Leroy and Mr. Gresham were innocent. I am informed that Mr. Leroy refused to tell exactly where he was at the time this crime was committed. Had he been guilty he would have had a previously prepared and perfectly plausible alibi. Then Mr. Gresham said frankly that he didn't know where he was at the particular hour about which Mr. Landon questioned him. Had he been the criminal, and left his handkerchief behind him by way of evidence, he, too, would have prearranged a story to tell glibly of his whereabouts. No, a perfect alibi should ordinarily lead to grave suspicion of the man making it, for it is ordinarily a concocted fiction. Again, it would have been a strange coincidence had your watch happened to run down, which you admit is a most unusual circumstance, at the only time in your whole life when you had a reason for its doing so. Your watch did not run down; you pretended that it did so as to get an opportunity to fix the time—the apparent time—in the mind of the hall boy at your apartment. This is what you did: You returned to your apartment much later than 11.25. In the absence of the boy, probably while he was up with the elevator, you stepped in and changed the time on the office clock. You went out again, and after a moment came in as if just reaching home. You then asked the boy the time, and he told you, although he had supposed it to be much later. Again you overdid your work when, while going up in the elevator, you asked the boy again, as if to make sure of the time, but really to fix it firmly in his mind, that he might witness for you. Some time later, during the night, you probably slipped down-stairs, eluding the elevator, and corrected the clock. All this is corroborated by the fact of your calling Miss Waring's attention to the time when you left her house. You carefully brought to her notice that it was then exactly eleven o'clock, which it was."

George Lawrence sat as if petrified; for the moment I think he was really more amazed at Fleming Stone's marvellous discoveries than alarmed at his own danger. He did not attempt to deny what Stone had said; indeed, he could not, for under the peculiar magnetism of the speaker's gaze Lawrence seemed hypnotized, and his silence had tacitly affirmed each point as it was brought out against him.

Suddenly he drew himself together with a bold shrug, as if preparing for a last desperate effort.

"Your deductions are true in part," he said. "I did change the clock, as you so diabolically discovered, and I suppose I did overdo matters when I accounted for every minute too carefully. But, though it was a manufactured alibi, and though I had reasons of my own for wanting to account for my movements that night, it has nothing to do with Robert Pembroke's death, and couldn't have had; for, as you all know, though I have a latch-key, the door was chained all night."

"Leaving that question, for a moment," said Fleming Stone, "let us consider these clues, which though apparently leading in various directions, point, Mr. Lawrence, directly and indubitably to yourself. When I was told by Mr. Landon of the several clues picked up in Mr. Pembroke's bedroom, the morning after his murder, I was impressed at once by their number and variety. It was extraordinary to find so many objects, unrecognized by any member of the household, in the murdered man's bedroom. Then, when I learned that some of these had been traced, and each so-called clue led to a different suspect, I saw at once that the situation was prearranged. The various clues were placed where they were found, exactly as a mine is 'salted' in expectation of prospectors. You, Mr. Lawrence, deliberately and with intent to throw suspicion in various directions, and thus baffle detectives,—you placed this key, this handkerchief, this time-table, and these torn tickets in the room where they were found. All this shows not only cleverness and ingenuity, but carefully prearranged plans. Where you obtained those precious 'clues,' I do not know, but at a guess I should venture to say that you picked up the ticket stubs in the street, as they show evidences of pavement dirt. The time-table has a distinct imprint of the roughened surface of the steel stair-binding. I think that as you came up the stairs, intent upon your deadly errand, you chanced to find that time-table, and left it behind you as one more distracting piece of evidence. But these details are of no importance. You salted the mine successfully, and by the diversity of your clues you led the honest efforts of the detectives in devious paths. But, after all, the missing money and the pin, used as a weapon, are the real clues. We have traced the pin,—to you. We have traced the money,—to you. We have eliminated all possible suspicion of anyone else, and if you have anything to say by way of defense, or in any way concerning the matter, you may speak now."

"I have only to say," said Lawrence, "that you have exhibited a marvelous ingenuity in building up this fabrication of falsehoods, but your whole structure falls to the ground in face of the positive evidence of the chain on the door. For though I have a latch key to the apartment, entrance is impossible when the chain bolt is on."

154

"Oh," cried Janet, with a wail as of utter despair. "If your alibi is broken, George, then I know how you got in that door!"

It was my turn to feel despair. Since the alibi was broken, Janet was practically confessing her complicity in the matter.

"What do you mean, Janet?" said George sharply. "I couldn't get in unless you had let me in, and you didn't."

"No," said Janet quietly; "I didn't. Nor did Charlotte. But I know how you got in—at least, how you could have got in."

"I, too, know how you got into the apartment," said Fleming Stone; "and it was without the assistance, and without the knowledge, of either Miss Pembroke or her servant."

Again that wonderful gaze of Fleming Stone's sad, serious eyes seemed to compel Lawrence to speak against his will.

"How did I get in?" he said hoarsely, bending forward as with the breathless suspense of a man taking his last chance.

"It is not an easy matter to explain," said Fleming Stone, "nor can I show the method in this apartment; but if you will all come with me across the hall, I will demonstrate to you the possibility of entering a chained door."

Without a word, we all crossed the hall and entered the Pembroke apartment. It was a cheerful, sunny suite of rooms, and its beautiful furniture and appointments seemed meant for a happy home life rather than grim tragedy. Fleming Stone went first, followed by Laura and George Lawrence. I followed with Janet, and, emboldened by her look of pathetic appeal, I clasped her hand in mine. When we were all inside Fleming Stone closed the door, the night-latch of which, of course, snapped itself.

Lawrence still acted as one hypnotized. Seemingly with no volition of his own, he followed Fleming Stone's movements, keeping his eyes fixed upon the detective as if literally unable to look elsewhere.

After closing the door, Fleming Stone put on the night-chain. For the first time I looked at the chain carefully. It was a heavy brass chain, long enough, when the door was closed, for the end, on which was a sort of knob or button, to reach back to the opening provided for it, and then slide along the brass slot until it stopped at the other end and hung in a loop. It seemed to me no different from dozens of chains I had seen of the same sort.

When it hung finally in position, Fleming Stone turned the knob and opened the door with a jerk, precisely as Charlotte had done on that memorable morning.

"Is it not true," asked Mr. Stone, "that this door, with the chain on thus, has often been violently jerked open?"

"Yes," said Janet; "Charlotte is very strong, and always pulls the door open sharply, forgetting the chain is there. And, too, Uncle Robert has often done the same thing, and his motions were always so vigorous that I thought sometimes he would break the chain."

"There was no danger of breaking the chain," said Mr. Stone; "but the repeated jerks at it have so forced the end of the slot nearest the edge of the door, that the brass is sprung outward, and the knob on the end of the chain may be removed—not as easily as it can be at the other end, it is true, but with some ingenious handling."

As he spoke, Fleming Stone, by some clever exertion, so twisted the knob on the end of the chain that it came out of the near end of the slot, with no necessity of pushing it back to the other end. I saw at once that this could be done also from the outside of the door, there being ample room when the door was ajar to slip one's hand in and free the chain in this manner.

At this demonstration of an actual fact, Fleming Stone did not look at George Lawrence, but at Miss Pembroke.

"You knew of this?" he said.

"I feared it," replied Janet, and I think she would not have spoken but for those impelling eyes upon her. "I remember George was out one evening when he was living here, and I thoughtlessly put the chain on the door and went to bed. The next morning, when I found that he had let himself in in some way, I wondered at it, but concluded that I must have been mistaken, and had not put the chain on. But I had noticed myself that the slot was sprung at this end, and I had been thinking that I would get a new and heavier chain bolt."

My first thought was that Janet's puzzling demeanor was now explained, and I understood why she had so readily accepted my services. She had suspected George from the first, because she knew that with his latch-key and the defective chain-lock he could make his entrance. But his perfect alibi had deceived her, and relieved her fear, so that she was glad or sad according as his alibi was sustained or doubted. Janet's evidence, of course, left no doubt as to George's guilt.

He saw this himself, and, seemingly at the end of his resources, he exclaimed: "It's no use. I may as well confess. I did kill Uncle Robert, but it was not premeditated, or, at least, not until a few moments before the deed. I want to make my confession to my cousin. I owe it to no one else."

But although Lawrence said this, he never once moved his eyes from Fleming Stone's face, and seemed really to make his confession to him.

"It was a violet pin I used, not a hat-pin. I—I had it, by accident, in my coat lapel all Wednesday afternoon at the matinée. On account of disastrous losses in Wall Street that morning, I had determined to kill myself. I'm not of much account, any way, and I was desperate. I knew Uncle Robert would give me no money to repay my stock losses, for he always thought speculation no better than any other sort of gambling—and it isn't. As I sat in the theatre, unconsciously my fingers trifled with the pin, and I conceived a notion of using that to take my own life, instead of a revolver. I went home to dress for dinner, and, still having the pin in my mind, I transferred it from my frock coat to my evening coat. As I stood looking at it while in my room, it occurred to me that were it not for the head of the pin I might push it into my flesh so far as to hide it. It would then be assumed, I thought, that I had died a natural death, and both the family and my memory would be saved the stigma of suicide. Acting on this thought, I laid the pin on the hearthstone and crushed off its glass head with my heel. Without definite intention as to when or where I should carry out my plan, I put the pin in my coat and went on to Miss Waring's dinner. It was as I sat at the dinner table, and looked around at other men of my own age and class, that I suddenly realized I did not want to give up a life which held promise of many years of pleasure, could I but tide over my financial troubles. I knew, too, that at Uncle Robert's death I should inherit enough to make good my losses, and an ample fortune besides. It was then, I think, that the thought came to me, why should not Uncle Robert die instead of myself? He was old, he had no joy in life, he made my cousin's life a burden to her, and his death would free us both from his tyranny. I'm not saying this by way of excuse or palliation, but simply to tell you how it occurred. Like a flash I realized that if my own death by means of the headless pin might be attributed to natural causes, the same would be true of Uncle Robert's death. I knew I could get into the apartment in the same way I had done before, and I knew, too, that as the chain slot was even more pulled out of shape now than it was then, I could with some manipulation replace the chain before closing the door. I think I need not say that I had no thought of implicating my cousin, for I had no thought of the pin being discovered. The idea obsessed me. The deed seemed inevitable. My brain was especially active, and planned the details with almost superhuman ingenuity. I left Miss Waring's at eleven o'clock, calling her attention to the fact purposely. I walked over here rather slowly, planning as I walked. I resolved, as Mr. Stone has remarked, to leave a misleading clue or two behind me. I searched the pavement as I walked, for something that would answer my purpose, and was surprised to see how little may be gleaned along a New York street. I found the two ticket stubs, evidently thrown away by someone, and put them in my pocket. Near here, less than two blocks away, I saw a shining object on the sidewalk, and picked up a key, which I was more than surprised to have traced to Mr. Leroy. I suppose he dropped it when he was hanging around here, beneath my cousin's window, on his way to the midnight train. I then came on to this house, and, after loitering about a minute in the street, I saw the elevator begin to rise. The main front door is always open, and I came in and walked up-stairs. It is easy to evade the elevator, even if it passes. On the stairs I found the time-table. And then I came——"

Lawrence stopped. Even his hardy bravado and indomitable will gave way before the picture that now came into his mind. His swaggering narrative ceased. His eyes fell, his mouth drooped, and he seemed on the verge of collapse.

Fleming Stone's quiet, even voice broke the silence. "And the handkerchief?" he said.

"It came in my laundry, by mistake," answered Lawrence, and he spoke like an automaton, his intelligence seeming to hang on the will of Fleming Stone.

"You brought it with you on purpose?"

"No; not that. When I left home my plans were entirely different, as I have told you. But I picked up the handkerchief hastily, and though noticing it was not my own, I thrust it into my pocket without thinking much about it."

"And then when you wanted evidence to incriminate some one other than yourself, you thought of those unknown initials, and flung the handkerchief on the bed."

"Yes," said Lawrence, still as if hypnotized by Stone's compelling glance.

"And afterwards——?"

"Afterwards—afterwards—I went out and got down-stairs the same way, having waited until the elevator was on the floor above. I felt like a man in a dream, but I knew that now I must establish my alibi. This I did exactly as Mr. Stone has described. I took great chances in tampering with the office clock, but I knew the boy to be of a stupid, dull-witted type, and, too, he was always half asleep during night hours. Again I watched my chance to elude the elevator, and slipped down-stairs later to set the clock right again. I suppose I overdid it in asking the boy the time twice, and also in drawing attention to the clock when it struck eleven."

"That is so," said Fleming Stone. "A perfect alibi is not possible unless it is a true one, and then it proves itself without any effort of anybody."

But all this happened many years ago. It is indeed a painful

158

memory, but time has blended away its poignancy. George Lawrence was arrested, but found the means to take his own life before his trial could be begun. Janet being left with a large fortune, went abroad at once and Laura accompanied her. The two became close friends, and when, some months later, I joined them in Italy, the course of true love began to run smoothly, and has continued to do so ever since.

Nor has it been difficult to understand Janet. For all queerness and contradictoriness disappeared after the mystery was solved. It was all because she suspected her cousin that she had endeavored to suppress any evidence that might throw suspicion toward him. He had asked her to get money for him from Robert Pembroke. She had asked her uncle for this, and he had told her that if she'd marry Leroy, he would give her not only the money she asked for, but much more. Knowing, as she did, of the defective bolt, she knew there was grave reason to suspect George both of murder and robbery. But once convinced of his alibi, she hoped the guilt might be placed elsewhere.

Also, of course, the life she led with her erratic and ill-tempered uncle affected her spirits, and made her lose temporarily the joyful and happy disposition that was really her own, and that was permanently restored after new scenes and new friends had caused her to forget the dreadful past.

Janet has been my wife for many years now, and, though we live in New York, our home is far removed from the Hammersleigh; and though our door is securely locked, we have never had it guarded by what was to Fleming Stone a chain of evidence.

www.ingramcontent.com/pod-product-compliance
Lightning Source LLC
Chambersburg PA
CBHW011506170626
46812CB00008B/2994